FOREVER FLOWING

Forever Flowing

Vasily Grossman

Translated from the Russian by Thomas P. Whitney

PERENNIAL LIBRARY

Harper & Row, Publishers, New York
Cambridge, Philadelphia, San Francisco
London, Mexico City, São Paulo, Singapore, Sydney

A hardcover edition of this book was published by Harper & Row, Publishers, Inc.

This book was first published in the Russian language under the title *Vse Techet*. World © 1970 *Possev-Verlag,* V. Gorachek KG, Frankfurt am Main.

Portions ("Quiet Mashenka") previously appeared in the Russian language in the November 1970 issue of *Possev.* World © Possev-Verlag, V. Gorachek KG, Frankfurt am Main.

A portion of the English translation has appeared in *Atlas* magazine.

 For information address Harper & Row, Publishers, Inc., 10 East 53rd Street, New York, N.Y. 10022. Published simultaneously in Canada by Fitzhenry & Whiteside Limited, Toronto.

First PERENNIAL LIBRARY edition published 1986.

Library of Congress Cataloging-in-Publication Data

Grossman, Vasiliĭ Semenovich.
Forever flowing.

Translation of: Vse techet.
I. Whitney, Thomas P. II. Title.
PG3476.G7V813 1986 891.73'42 85-45341
ISBN 0-06-091317-7 (pbk.)

---

86 87 88 89 90 MPC 10 9 8 7 6 5 4 3 2 1

Forever Flowing

1

The Khabarovsk express was due in Moscow at 9 A.M. A young man in pajamas was scratching his shaggy head and gazing out the window into the dim light of the autumn dawn. He yawned and addressed himself to the other passengers waiting there in the aisle with their soap dishes and towels:

"Well, citizens, who's last in line?"

He was told that his place in the queue was behind a portly citizeness who had temporarily absented herself and who in turn was behind the chap who was clinging to a squeezed-out tube of toothpaste and a well-worn cake of soap plastered over with scraps of newspaper.

The young man took it upon himself to declaim: "Why is only one of the washrooms open? After all, we are arriving at our destination, the capital. But the conductors have only one thing on their minds: counting their money. They couldn't care less about what the passengers need."

The fat woman wearing a bathrobe returned to her place in line after a few minutes, and the young man said to her:

"Citizeness, I'm after you. For now, I'm going back to my compartment rather than dawdle around here in the aisle."

Back in his compartment the young man opened his orange suitcase and admired his possessions. Three men shared the compartment with him. One, the back of whose head was broad and bulbous, was snoring away. A second, ruddy, bald, and young, was busy rearranging papers in his briefcase. And the third was a thin and silent old man who sat staring out the window with his forehead resting on his swarthy fist.

The young man addressed his ruddy traveling companion: "Have you finished my book? I have to pack it."

What he really wanted was for the other man to look at and admire his suitcase and its contents: rayon shirts, swimming trunks, dark glasses in white frames, and a copy of *The Concise Philosophical Dictionary*. And off to one side, covered with a small-town newspaper, were some dry gray shortbreads of a kind baked nowadays only in the country.

The ruddy young man handed back the book: "Here, take it! *Eugénie Grandet*. I discovered I read it last year at a resort."

"It's really a strong bit of writing, you have to admit that," pronounced the shaggy young man and put the book in his suitcase.

They had passed the time during their long journey playing cards, drinking, eating, discussing movies and records, furniture, socialist agriculture and the like, and in arguing which soccer team had the better offensive—Spartak or Dynamo.

The ruddy bald fellow was a trade-union inspector in a provincial capital. The shaggy young man, who was returning to Moscow after spending his vacation in a farming area, worked as an economist on the State Planning Commission for the Russian Republic.

The traveler with the broad, bulbous cranium, who continued to snore away in the lower berth, was a Siberian construction superintendent. He had greatly displeased the economist and the trade-union inspector with his bad manners. He cursed freely and belched after meals. And when he discovered that one of his companions worked in the department of the State Planning Commission, which was concerned with theoretical economics—political economy—he had commented:

"Political economy—now that's about collective farmers traveling from the country to the city to buy up bread from the workers, right?"

Then once he had gotten drunk in a station bar and buffet where he had gone, as he expressed it, "to check in." And he kept everyone in the compartment awake most of the night with the racket he raised:

"In the construction business you'll get nowhere by obeying the law. If you're going to fulfill the plan, you have to get out and scramble and do whatever you have to do. The principle is: 'You scratch my back and I'll scratch yours.' Under the czars they used to call it private enterprise, and the way we put it is: 'You've got to let a man live; a man has to live.' That's real economics! On my construction project welders were on the payroll as nursery school teachers for a whole quarter, until we were able to get new appropriations. The law flies in the face of life—but life makes its demands anyway! Fulfill the plan, they insist. They offer you a bonus and prize money—and they can just as easily slap a ten-year sentence on you too. The law goes against life and life goes against the law."

The two younger men kept silent. But when the construction boss fell to snoring loudly, they expressed their opinions:

"People like that should be investigated. They only pretend to be loyal!"

"A fixer! No principles! Some sort of kike!"

And what really made them mad was that this crude, and yet not shallow, man held them in contempt. He said once: "There were prisoners on my construction job. They used to call people like you 'trusties,' and 'parasites.' But when the time comes to decide who built Communism, you'll be right there to put in your claim."

And with that he had gone off to another compartment to play cards.

It was clear that the fourth traveler had rarely if ever been in a reserved-seat "soft" car, with compartments and real bunks. He spent most of his journey just sitting there, elbows on knees as if anxious to cover up the patches on his pants. The sleeves of his black sateen shirt were too short, ending midway between his wrists and elbows. White buttons on the collar and chest gave the shirt a sort of childish look—as if a boy should be wearing it. It was somehow amusing and touching to see children's buttons on a man with graying temples, with the fatigued and troubled eyes of old age.

The construction superintendent said to him in a voice accustomed to ordering people about: "Come on there, daddy, get away from the table. I want to have tea!"

And the old man jumped up like a soldier obeying an order and went out into the aisle.

Inside the old man's plywood suitcase, with its peeling paint, a loaf of crumbling bread lay alongside his laundered linen. And after he had rolled himself a cigarette of the strong, coarse Russian tobacco called makhorka he would go out on the car platform to puff away—so as not to annoy his compartment mates with the stinking fumes.

Now and then his companions would treat him to salami, and once the construction boss brought him a hard-boiled egg and a glass of vodka. Even those passengers half his age insisted on addressing him—as they would an inferior or a child—with the condescending, even insulting, familiar pronoun. And the construction boss kept joking about how "old daddy" would say he was single when he got to Moscow and find himself a young wife.

One time in the compartment the talk got on the subject of collective farms, whereupon the young economist began to berate "village loafers."

"I've seen it now with my own eyes. Every morning they gather at the farm administration building and keep milling around and scratching their heads. All sorts of time gets lost before the farm chairman and the brigadiers pack them off to work. And then they keep complaining that under Stalin they got nothing for their workdays on the farm and that even now they still get practically nothing."

The trade-union inspector, thoughtfully shuffling a deck of cards, seconded him: "What should they be paid for, friends, if they don't fulfill the plan for deliveries to the state? They need to be taught—like this!"

And he shook a big white peasant fist in the air—a fist long since unaccustomed to manual labor.

And the construction boss just stroked his fat chest with its rows of greasy ribbons representing government decorations. "At the front we had bread. The Russian people fed us. And no one had to teach them to do it either."

"Now you're right about that," said the economist. "No matter what, the most important thing is that we are Russians. It's no small thing to be a Russian!"

The trade-union inspector smiled and winked broadly at his companion: "In other words, as they say: 'The Russian is the elder brother and first among equals!' Right?"

"That's what makes you mad," blurted the young economist. "After all, we are talking about Russians, not Germans! One of them harangued me: 'We had to live on linden leaves for five whole years and from 1947 on we got nothing at all for our workdays on the collective farm.' They don't like to work. They simply won't understand that nowadays everything depends on the people."

And he looked over at the graying old fellow who was listening and saying nothing and said: "You musn't be angry, daddy. If you don't do your duty at work, the government puts you on its black list."

"What can you do with them?" remarked the construction boss. "They've got no conscience at all! They want to eat every day!"

Like the majority of railway car conversations, this one, too, ended nowhere. An air force major with gold teeth shining brightly stuck his head into their compartment and said to the younger men reproachfully: "How about it, comrades? What about getting down to work?"

And they went off to a nearby compartment to finish up a card game.

And now the long, long journey was coming to its end. The passengers were packing their slippers into their suitcases and leaving on the compartment tables pieces of stale bread, half-eaten bluish chicken bones, and tail ends of salami wrapped in their aging skins.

The sullen women conductors had gathered up the crushed and rumpled bedding and disappeared.

Soon, soon the world of the transcontinental railway car would scatter. Jokes, faces, laughter would be forgotten, and with them life stories and personal tragedies recounted casually or in a weak moment.

Ever closer moved the enormous city, capital of a mighty state. The thoughts and concerns of the journey lay behind them. Forgotten were the conversations with a fellow passenger in the vestibule of the car, while beyond the dirty window glass the enormous Russian plain kept rolling past before one's eyes, and the water in the car tanks kept sloshing back and forth behind one's back.

The closely knit world of the railway car, which had come into being so swiftly—and was, by virtue of its own laws, the equal of all the other people-created worlds which move in straight and crooked lines through space and time—was already melting away.

Great is the power of the enormous city. It quickens even the feckless hearts of those who have come to the capital merely as tourists, to wander about the stores and to go to the zoo and the planetarium. Every person who falls into the powerful magnetic field within which stretch this world-renowned city's taut, invisible lines of force experiences sudden confusion and anguish.

The economist nearly missed his place in line at the bathroom. When he returned, still combing his hair on the run, he seated himself in the compartment, and looked at his fellow passengers.

The construction boss was rearranging his sheets of cost projections with trembling fingers—for the drinking had been heavy on this journey.

The trade-union inspector had already put on his jacket

and lapsed into silence—he had grown timid as he fell into the magnetic field of human disarray. He was thinking how that bilious gray-haired old witch in charge of trade-union inspectors was certainly going to have words with him.

The train hurtled past village log cabins and brickworks, past tin-gray cabbage fields, past station platforms with gray puddles on their asphalt from the overnight rains. Upon those platforms stood the stolid people of the Moscow suburbs with plastic raincapes over their coats. Beneath gray clouds dangled high-tension power lines. And on station sidings stood sinister gray freight cars labeled: "Slaughterhouse Station, Terminal Railway."

And with a kind of malicious, ever-increasing speed, the train thundered forward. That kind of speed levels out and cleaves apart space and time.

The old man sat at the table, his fists tight against his temples, looking out the window.

Many years earlier a young man with a shaggy, tousled mat of hair had sat just like this at the window of a third-class passenger coach. The people who had been traveling with him then had all disappeared; their faces, their voices had been forgotten. And yet, within that gray head, something had once again come to life which one would have supposed had totally ceased to exist.

The train had already entered the green belt around Moscow. The gray tatters of smoke grasped at the fir branches and, forced downward by the air currents, flowed across the tops of country house fences. How very familiar were the silhouettes of those austere northern firs. How strange beside them looked the blue pointed picket fences, the sharp-pointed country house gables, the varicolored windowpanes of country house verandas, and the flowerbeds with their lush dahlias.

And the man who for three decades had forgotten that clumps of lilacs still existed in the world—or beds of pansies, or garden paths sprinkled with sand, or carts from which vendors sold carbonated soft drinks—this man sighed deeply, seeing once again, this time under a new aspect, that life had gone on without him.

2

Nikolai Andreyevich read through the telegram the delivery boy had just handed him—and for a moment regretted the tip he had given him. The name signed at the bottom seemed to be a stranger's; it was obvious the telegram had been delivered to the wrong address. But all of a sudden he realized—and he cried out in his surprise. It was from his first cousin, Ivan.

"Masha! Masha!" he summoned his wife.

Mariya Pavlovna took the telegram, only to complain: "You know I can't read a thing without my reading glasses. Go get them."

"They aren't very likely to give him permission to live in Moscow," she said after she had read it.

"Why do you have to talk about that?" He passed his hand across his brow and declared: "Just think, how awful! Vanya is coming and he'll find nothing but graves, just graves."

Mariya Pavlovna knitted her brows and said: "This is going to be terribly embarrassing with the Sokolovs. Of course we can send them our birthday gift, but even then it's most unfortunate that we'll not be there. It is, after all, his fiftieth birthday party."

"Don't worry—I'll explain. He'll understand."

"No doubt, and the news that Ivan has returned and come straight here from the railway station will go straight from the birthday party all over Moscow."

Nikolai Andreyevich shook the telegram right in her face. "Can't you really understand how dear to me Vanya is?"

He was irritated with his wife. All the petty considerations to which she had given utterance had entered his own mind before she spoke a word. It often happened that way. His outburst had really resulted from seeing his own weaknesses in her. But he failed to grasp this fact. Just as he could not realize that he always forgave his wife so swiftly and easily after their quarrels precisely because in forgiving her he was really forgiving himself—whom he loved so much.

Yes, that very same silly thought about the Sokolovs' birthday party had entered his own mind.

The truth was that the news of Ivan's arrival had shocked him so deeply because it caused his own life, full of truth and untruth, right and wrong, to rise up before him.

He was ashamed to have had even momentary regrets because he would be missing the formal dinner at the Sokolovs, missing the Sokolovs' friendly decanter of vodka. He was ashamed of the pettiness of his initial reactions. The thought had flashed through his mind, too, that Ivan might put him to a good deal of trouble to arrange permission for him to reside in Moscow. He, too, had shrunk from the thought that Ivan's return might become common knowledge in Moscow and have a harmful effect on his chances in the impending elections to the Academy.

But Mariya Pavlovna kept right on tormenting Nikolai Andreyevich by uttering the thoughts he himself had had and suppressed. She insisted on bringing them out into the open.

"I don't understand you at all!" he exclaimed. "You make me feel as if I could only rejoice in this good news by not sharing it with you."

His words hurt her. But she knew Nikolai Andreyevich would nonetheless embrace her immediately and say: "Masha, Masha, we will enjoy it together! How else?"

And that was what he said. So she stood there with a patient little frown on her face, which was her way of replying: "I'm not in the least delighted by your tender words, but I will be patient."

Then their eyes met and love wiped out the irritation.

For twenty-eight years they had lived together inseparably. And it is not easy to grasp and analyze the relations of people who have lived together for nearly a third of a century.

So now she, gray-headed, went to the window and watched him, gray-headed, get into the car. And there had been a time when they used to dine in a student dining hall on Bronnaya Street!

"Kolya, Kolya," said Mariya Pavlovna quietly, "just think: Ivan never saw our Valya. He was arrested before Valya came into the world, and now that he has finally returned, Valya has been eight years in his grave."

And the thought astounded her.

3

Nikolai Andreyevich sat waiting for his cousin—and thought about his own life and prepared himself to repent of it to Ivan.

He imagined how he would show him through the apartment. There in the dining room was a fine Oriental rug. Beautiful, isn't it? Masha has good taste—Ivan, at any rate, did not have to be told who her father had been in old St. Petersburg. Good Lord, they had really known how to live in those days!

And how would he set about talking with Ivan? He wondered. Whole decades had passed, a whole lifetime. But no, the whole point would be that life was not over, that it was only now beginning.

What a meeting it would be! Ivan was arriving at such an astonishing time. How many changes there had been since Stalin! Everyone had been touched by them. Workers, and the peasants too. Bread was available. Ivan had returned from camp—and not Ivan alone. And in Nikolai Andreyevich's life a turning point had come—a very important one.

Nikolai Andreyevich, for long years of his career, going back all the way to his university days, had failed to achieve major recognition as a scientist. This tormented him all the more because he felt it was unfair. He had a good education. He worked hard. He was considered a fine raconteur. Women fell for him.

He was very proud of having a reputation as an honest man of principle, and at the same time he was hostile to pious hypocrisy. He enjoyed amusing anecdotes at dinner, knew his way about in the vintage years of dry wines, and used frequently to bypass the wine and move on to vodka.

His acquaintances praised his character now and then, but when they did, Mariya Pavlovna, with her gay and angry eyes fixed on her husband, would exclaim: "You think he's so wonderful. You ought to live with him and then you would find out all about him: Kolya, the despot, the psychopath, an egotist the likes of which the world has never known."

Often enough she and her husband really did irritate each other beyond all limits because of their mutual knowledge of each other's weaknesses and faults. There had been times when it seemed that it might be easier to part than to continue. But it had only seemed that way. They really couldn't live without each other—or at any rate if they had parted, each would have suffered keenly.

Mariya Pavlovna was a mere schoolgirl when she had fallen in love with Nikolai Andreyevich. All the things about him which had seemed to her astonishing and wonderful thirty years before—his voice, his prominent forehead, his big teeth, his smile—had, as the years passed, become even dearer to her.

He loved her too, but his love had changed. And what had once been the main thing in their relationship had now retired into the background, while what had once seemed less significant had come to the fore.

Mariya Pavlovna, dark-eyed and tall, had once been pretty. Even now her gestures had a distinctive airiness and grace, and her eyes had not lost the loveliness of youth. But the feature which in youth had marred her beauty—her large lower teeth which stuck out when she smiled—had become even more prominent with age.

Nikolai Andreyevich's failure to win recognition had been a source of deep pain to him. Even back in their university seminars, it had not been his meticulously prepared reports but the impromptu comments of the red-headed Rodionov or the drunkard Pyzhov that had excited the others.

Nikolai had gone on to become a senior research scientist in a famous scientific institute. He had published dozens of articles in learned journals. He had successfully defended his doctoral dissertation. Yet he had suffered torments and humiliations of which only his wife knew.

At the heart of his branch of science stood a handful of men. One was a member of the Academy of Sciences; two had positions of lower rank than Nikolai Andreyevich's; one of them had never won his degree as a doctoral candidate. All of them appreciated Nikolai Andreyevich as a conversationalist with whom it was pleasant to pass the time of day. They esteemed his decency. But very sincerely and good-naturedly they considered him a zero as a scientist.

He was constantly aware of the atmosphere of tension and excitement surrounding these men, especially the lame Mandelshtam.

A London scientific journal had once described Mandelshtam as "the scientist who superbly carries on the principles of the founders of contemporary biology." When Nikolai Andreyevich read this phrase, he really felt that if he could only have read such words about himself he would have died of sheer joy.

Mandelshtam, to be sure, behaved badly. Sometimes he was gloomy and depressed. Sometimes he took a haughty, overbearing tone. On certain occasions, at some get-together, when he had had a drink or two, he would mimic scientists he knew. He would go so far as to call them dullards or worse—forgers, plagiarists, thieves. This habit angered Nikolai Andreyevich because Mandelshtam was pouring out his scorn on people whose hospitality he had enjoyed. And Nikolai Andreyevich used to imagine how Mandelshtam would, no doubt, call him, Nikolai Andreyevich, a nonentity and a thief behind his back.

Mandelshtam's wife angered him too—she was a fat woman who once upon a time had been good-looking and who nowadays, it seemed, cared only about playing cards for money and the fame of her lame scientist husband.

At the same time, Nikolai Andreyevich was very drawn to Mandelshtam, and he often used to say that life must be difficult for such brilliant and special people.

Yet when it happened that Mandelshtam would condescendingly tick him off, Nikolai Andreyevich grew very angry indeed and was in torment. And when he arrived home, he would let off steam and curse Mandelshtam as an upstart.

Mariya Pavlovna considered her husband a man of great talent. And the more Nikolai Andreyevich told her of the condescending indifference to him and his work on the part of the great men in his field, the stronger and more fanatical grew her faith in him. And he needed her faith in him and her excitement about his work just as a drunkard needs vodka. His own attitude was that success came easily to some people and to some it just didn't, some were lucky and others were unlucky—but by and large everyone was much the same. Mandelshtam, as he saw it, had been marked by some special good luck. He was a kind of Benjamin the Fortunate in biology. And, as Nikolai Andreyevich envisioned it, Rodionov, like some leading operatic tenor, was surrounded by his claque, his fans. Of course, snub-nosed Rodionov, with his prominent high cheekbones, bore very little resemblance to a popular operatic tenor. And, as Nikolai Andreyevich saw it, Isaac Khavkin was another lucky individual—though he had never received his degree as a doctoral candidate and though he was blacklisted for employment in any scientific institute or other important institution—even in the most relaxed of times—because he was suspected of the heresy of vitalism. As a result, Khavkin, a gray-haired man, worked in a local public health bacteriological laboratory where he went about in patched-up britches. But academicians used to go there to consult him. And in his pitiful little lab he was carrying on research which was the subject of intense scientific interest and discussion.

When the campaign against the Weismannists and Mendelians began, the severity of the disciplinary measures meted out to many of his fellow biologists made Nikolai Andreyevich very sad. He and Mariya Pavlovna were both very disappointed when Rodionov refused to confess his errors and was fired. Nikolai Andreyevich regarded his quixotic courage as reprehensible, but worked out arrangements for him to do translations from English anyway.

Pyzhov in the meantime was charged with toadying to Western bourgeois science and packed off to a post in an experimental laboratory in remote Chkalov Province. Nikolai Andreyevich wrote to him and sent him books. And Mariya Pavlovna assembled gift parcels for the family and sent them off for the New Year.

In the papers an avalanche of articles began to appear with one basic theme. They exposed careerists and thieves who had won diplomas by plagiarism and deceit, physicians guilty of criminal cruelty to sick mothers and children, engineers who had built country houses for themselves and their kinfolk instead of schools and hospitals. The common denominator was that almost all those exposed in these articles appeared to be Jewish, and the papers took special pains to report their names and patronymics in order to make sure that their readers understood this: "Srul Nakhmanovich, Khaim Abramovich, Izrail Mendelevich . . ." There were reviews attacking books by Jewish writers—and if the writer in question used a Russian pseudonym, then his original Jewish name would be given in parentheses. It was a time when one might have gotten the impression that in the entire U.S.S.R. only Jews were engaged in thievery, or bribe-taking, or were criminally negligent of the sufferings of patients, or were writing bad books.

Nikolai Andreyevich could certainly observe that these articles were giving great joy not only to janitors and drunks on suburban trains. They outraged him—yet at the same time he was terribly irritated at his Jewish friends who seemed to feel all these scribblings meant the end of the world. They complained that talented young Jews were being denied admission to postgraduate courses, that Jews were not being accepted in the physics department of the university, that Jews were not being hired for official posts in ministries—not only in heavy industry but in light industry as well. They reported that young Jews who graduated from higher educational institutions were being assigned jobs in particularly remote areas, that whenever staff reductions were made it was almost always the Jews only who lost their jobs.

Of course, all this was quite true. Yet the Jews seemed to be obsessed with the idea that there was some kind of grandiose government plan to condemn them to persecution, starvation, and death. Nikolai Andreyevich, on the other hand, considered that what was involved was clearly a hostile attitude toward Jews among a segment of Party and government officialdom. It was out of the question, in his opinion, that there might be any written instructions to personnel departments and admissions committees concerning Jews. Stalin, he felt, was not an anti-Semite, and, no doubt, simply knew nothing about it.

And it was not only the Jews in his own field who were suffering either. Old Churkovsky, Pyzhov, and Rodionov had gotten their comeuppance too.

Mandelshtam, who had been in charge of the scientific department of the Institute, was demoted to being a mere staff member in the same department. He could continue with his work, and his doctor's degree brought him a large salary.

But then came the unsigned editorial in *Pravda* attacking a group of cosmopolite theater critics—Gurvich, Yuzovsky, and others—for mocking the Russian theater. And that began an intense campaign to expose cosmopolites in all areas of science and art, and Mandelshtam was declared an "anti-patriot." In an article in the wall newspaper posted in the Institute, doctoral candidate Bratova wrote: "On returning from his distant travels, Mark Samuilovich Mandelshtam cast into oblivion the principles of Soviet Russian science."

The upshot was that Nikolai Andreyevich went to call on Mandelshtam at his home, and the latter was touched and sad and his haughty wife was by no means so haughty any longer. They downed a bit of vodka together. Mandelshtam cursed Bratova, who had been his own student. He buried his hands in his shock of hair and grieved over his brilliant young Jewish students who were being driven out of science.

"What are they supposed to do now," he asked Nikolai Andreyevich, "sell haberdashery in stalls at the bazaars?"

"Oh, come now, don't be worried," replied the latter. "There's plenty of work for everyone—for you, for Khavkin, and even for the lab technician, Anichka Zilberman. You will all have bread—with caviar on it too," Nikolai Andreyevich said jokingly.

"Good heavens!" said Mandelshtam. "What makes you think it's a question of caviar? It's human dignity that's at stake."

And, as it turned out, Nikolai Andreyevich had been mistaken about Khavkin. Things had taken a bad turn for him. After the communiqué on the doctor-assassins had appeared in the newspaper, Khavkin had been arrested.

That communiqué, asserting that Jewish medical men and the actor Mikhoels had been guilty of monstrous crimes, shocked everyone. It seemed as though a dark cloud hung over Moscow, creeping into homes and schools and worming its way into human hearts.

The communiqué had been published on the last page of

the newspaper, under the heading "Chronicle." What it said was that all the accused doctors had confessed under interrogation—and this meant there was no shadow of a doubt of their guilt.

Yet the whole thing seemed unthinkable. It was very hard to go about one's work knowing that professors and academicians had turned out to be the assassins of Zhdanov and Shcherbakov, that they had become poisoners.

Whenever Nikolai Andreyevich recollected the kind Dr. Vovsi and the wonderful actor Mikhoels, the crimes with which they were charged seemed quite unimaginable.

But it was said that they had confessed. And if they were innocent but had confessed anyway, that implied another crime—a crime against them more monstrous than the one of which they were accused.

Even to think about this was frightening. It took bravery to doubt their guilt—because then the real criminals were the leaders of the socialist state. In that case, the real criminal was Stalin.

And meanwhile his doctor friends told Nikolai Andreyevich that it had become nearly impossible to carry on their work in the hospitals and polyclinics. The terrifying official announcement had made patients suspicious. Many refused to be treated by Jewish doctors. There was a mass of complaints and denunciations of allegedly intentional careless treatment. In pharmacies, druggists were suspected of trying to pass off poison as medicine. Tales were being told on streetcars, at markets, and at work—claiming that several Moscow pharmacies had been shut down because the druggists—Jews and American agents—had sold pills consisting of dried lice. Tales were told about babies and their mothers being infected with syphilis in maternity homes and patients being injected with cancer of the jaw and tongue in dental surgery clinics. There were even rumors circulating to the effect that ordinary boxes of matches with deadly poisons in them were being passed off on unsuspecting people.

Certain individuals recollected what they considered to be suspicious circumstances in the deaths of relatives long dead and sent statements to the security organs demanding the investigation and arrest of Jewish physicians. And the rumors were widely believed—not just by half-literate and half-drunken janitors, truck drivers, and stevedores, but by certain scientists, writers, engineers, and university students too.

Nikolai Andreyevich found the widespread mistrust impossible. At the Institute, the lab technician, large-nosed Anna Naumovna, would come in looking pale and with wide, half-crazed eyes. She reported one day that her apartment house neighbor had committed suicide in terror, leaving behind two orphans: a daughter studying at a musical institute and a schoolboy son. The woman, who worked in a pharmacy, had given a customer the wrong medicine in a fit of absent-mindedness. When she had been called in to explain what had happened, she simply could not face it.

Anna Naumovna now came to work on foot—to avoid drunken passengers in streetcars who tried to get her into conversation about the Jewish doctor-assassins who had murdered Zhdanov and Shcherbakov.

Nikolai Andreyevich found the new Institute Director, Ryskov, repulsive. Ryskov had been heard to say that the time had come to purge Russian science of non-Russian names. And on one occasion he had stated: "This is the end of the yid synagogue! How I hate them!"

And yet nonetheless Nikolai Andreyevich could not repress his involuntary pleasure at Ryskov's statement to him: "The comrades in the Central Committee are very appreciative of your work as a great Russian scientist."

Mandelshtam was no longer employed at the Institute. He had managed to get a job as a methodologist in a university lab. Nikolai Andreyevich made his wife phone the Mandelshtams to invite them to tea. But Mandelshtam was by this time on edge and suspicious. To tell the truth, Nikolai Andreyevich was glad Mark Samuilovich kept intentionally avoiding him—their encounters had become more and more unpleasant. In times like these one wished to be among cheerful people.

Nikolai Andreyevich, when he first heard of Khavkin's arrest, whispered to his wife while staring fearfully at the telephone: "I am certain Isaac is innocent. I have known him for thirty years."

Mariya Pavlovna quickly embraced him and stroked his head: "How proud of you I am! I am the only one who knows how much pain Khavkin and Mandelshtam have caused you—and how generous you are toward them!"

This was a difficult time, and Nikolai Andreyevich had to make a speech on vigilance and complacency at a meeting in the Institute about the doctor-assassins.

After the meeting was over, Nikolai Andreyevich spoke with Professor Margolin, a scientist in the physiochemistry department, who had also made one of the important speeches. Margolin had read the text of the congratulations to be sent to Lidiya Timashuk, the doctor who had exposed the doctor-assassins. And he had demanded the death penalty for the doctor-criminals. This Margolin was an adept in Marxist philosophy and was the instructor in the course on the fourth chapter of the *Short Course*—Stalin's exposition of the elements of dialectical materialism.

"Times are difficult, Samson Abramovich," said Nikolai Andreyevich. "It wasn't easy for me to speak on these matters, but it must have been even more difficult for you."

Margolin lifted his thin brows and pushed forward his pale lower lip, asking: "I beg your pardon. I am not quite certain what you have in mind."

"Well," replied Nikolai Andreyevich, "you know, Vovsi, Etinger, Kogan—just who could have imagined? I was a patient in Vovsi's clinic myself and I liked his people very much and his patients believed in him as if he were God."

Margolin wrinkled his pale, bloodless nostrils and lifted his thin shoulder a bit and said: "Ah, yes, I see. You consider it's unpleasant for me, a Jew, to condemn those monsters? On the contrary, Jewish nationalism is especially loathsome to me. And if Jews, because they like America, become obstacles on the road to Communism, then I would sacrifice not only myself but my own daughter to get rid of them."

Nikolai Andreyevich realized he had made a mistake in mentioning how much Vovsi's naïve patients had liked him. After all, if this man would not even spare his own daughter, then the only way to talk to him was in the language of trite official formulae.

And so he said: "By all means, of course. The doom of the enemy lies in our moral and political unity."

Yes, those times had been difficult, and the only comfort Nikolai Andreyevich found was that his work was going well.

For the first time he had burst his narrow confines and launched out into the vital areas to which he had previously been refused admittance. People began to come to him, to ask his advice, to be grateful for his responses. Scientific journals that had previously ignored him sought his articles. He even had a call from VOKS—the Society for Cultural Relations with Foreign Countries—an institution which had never before asked him for anything. They wanted the manuscript of his still unfinished book so they could take the initiative in getting it published in other Communist countries.

Nikolai Andreyevich was profoundly excited and touched by the arrival of his success at long last. Mariya Pavlovna was much more relaxed than he. In her eyes success was bound to come to her Kolyenka; so now it had.

Changes in Nikolai Andreyevich's life came one after another. The new people who ran the Institute had promoted him but they were not people he liked. He was repelled by their rudeness, extreme cockiness, readiness to attack scientific opponents as toadies, cosmopolites, imperialist hirelings, and capitalist agents. But he was still able to see the main thing in these people—audacity, courage, strength.

Mandelshtam had been wrong to call them illiterate idiots and "dogmatically narrow-minded young colts." It was not narrowness that characterized them but passion, a purposefulness that led to life and arose from life. That was why they hated hair-splitters, abstract theoreticians.

And they, the new chiefs of the Institute, though they sensed in Nikolai Andreyevich a man with views and ways different from their own, still had a positive attitude toward him and trusted him as a Russian. He got a warm letter from Lysenko, who praised his manuscript and offered a mutual-assistance pact.

Nikolai Andreyevich's position on Lysenko's theories was negative—which did not prevent his finding this letter from the famous academician and agronomist quite pleasing. Yes. And he considered that one could not simply reject all of Lysenko's work out of hand. And he considered that the rumors of his being very dangerous to his scientific opponents and resorting habitually to police methods and denunciations were, in all likelihood, exaggerated.

Ryskov asked Nikolai Andreyevich to make a speech denouncing the cosmopolites who had been driven out of the biological sciences, and Nikolai Andreyevich turned him down—though he could see how dissatisfied the director was. Ryskov wanted the public to hear the wrathful voice of a Russian scientist who was not a member of the Communist Party.

About this time rumors were circulating about the hurried construction of an enormous city of barracks in Siberia. It was said these barracks were being built for the Jews. They would be sent into exile just as the Kalmyks, the Crimean Tatars, the Bulgarians, the Greeks, the Volga Germans, and the Balkars and Chechens had been sent into exile.

By then Nikolai Andreyevich realized he had been wrong in predicting caviar sandwiches for Mandelshtam.

His concern grew as he waited for the trial of the doctor-assassins. Each morning he looked through the papers to learn whether it had already begun. Like everyone he was anxious to know whether it would be an open trial. He often asked Mariya Pavlovna: "What do you think? Will they publish a day-by-day report of the trial, with the prosecutor's speech, with questions and answers, with a chance for the defendants to make their own final statements? Or will there just be a communiqué from the Military Collegium?"

In the greatest secrecy Nikolai Andreyevich was told by a certain person that the way things would go was this: The doctors would be publicly executed on Red Square; a wave of pogroms against the Jews would roll through the whole country; this would be the signal for the exile of all the Jews to the taiga and to the Kara-Kum Desert to build the Turkmenian Canal. This exile would be undertaken in order to protect the Jews from the just but merciless wrath of the people. And it would be an expression of the eternally vital spirit of Soviet internationalism, which, while it appreciated and understood the people's wrath on the one hand, would nonetheless not permit mass kangaroo courts and repressions.

Like everything else that took place in the Soviet Union, this spontaneous wrath at the bloody crimes of the Jews was thought out ahead of time and planned in full detail.

In exactly the same way, the elections to the Supreme Soviet were planned ahead of time in full detail by Stalin. Secret meetings were held in advance and candidates were picked—and from that point on the spontaneous nomination of candidates took place on a planned and scheduled basis, as did the campaigning for them and, in the end, their victory in the national elections. In exactly the same way, stormy protest meetings were organized, and explosions of the people's wrath, or manifestations of brotherly friendship. And in exactly the same way, weeks in advance of the holiday parades, the texts of the reports from Red Square were approved: "At this very moment I am watching the rolling tanks." In exactly the same way, the personal innovations and achievements of such "shock troops" as Stakhanov, Izotov, and Dusya Vinogradova had been organized ahead of time. That was how the mass enlistment in the collective farms had been organized.

That was how the legendary heroes of the Civil War had been designated and then made to disappear. It was exactly how the workers came to demand that state loans be issued, and also to demand that they be permitted to work on their days off. That was exactly how all the nationwide love for the great leader and teacher had been organized.

That was how secret agents from abroad, spies, diversionists, wreckers, were suddenly discovered. That was how, at the end of the process of interrogation and complex cross-questioning, written confessions were signed by bookkeepers, engineers, attorneys and the like, admitting their manifold terrorist and espionage activities—though only a little while before they had never even suspected it themselves.

That was exactly how the letters came into being which wooden-voiced mothers read into microphones, appealing to their soldier sons. It was how the great patriotic wartime appeal of the collective farmer Ferapont Golovaty for contributions to the Red Army had been worked out ahead of time. It was how speakers spoke in "open, free discussions": the texts of their speeches had been prepared and approved ahead of time—for if, for some reason, "open, free discussions" were required, they had to be planned and organized in advance.

And then, suddenly, on March 5, 1953, Stalin died. His death dropped right into the middle of this whole gigantic system of mechanized enthusiasm, of mechanized wrath and mechanized love of the people, organized and designated on instructions from the district Party committees.

Stalin died without previous planning, without instructions from the administrative apparatus. Stalin died without the personal instructions of Comrade Stalin.

In this freedom and spontaneity, this capriciousness of death, there was something explosive, something contradictory to the innermost essence of the Soviet state. Confusion seized minds and hearts.

Stalin had died! Some were overcome with grief. There were certain schools in which the teachers compelled the pupils to get down on their knees and, kneeling themselves and shedding profuse tears, read aloud the government communiqué on the death of the leader. At mourning meetings in institutions and factories many were overcome with hysteria; there were insane cries and women sobbed. Some even fainted. The great god, the great stone image of the twentieth century, had died—and women wept.

Others were overcome with joy. The countryside which had groaned beneath the iron weight of Stalin's hand sighed with relief.

And the many millions in the camps celebrated.

Columns of prisoners marched out to work in deep darkness. The roar of the taiga drowned out the barking of the guard dogs. And then, in a moment, as if the northern lights had flashed the signal across their ranks, came the words: "Stalin is dead!" Tens of thousands of prisoners marching under guard passed the news along in whispers: "He's croaked, he's croaked." And this whisper of the thousands upon thousands roared like the wind. Black night hung over the arctic earth. But the ice in the Arctic Ocean had begun to break up and the ocean rumbled.

There were many in Russia—both educated people and workers—who felt a conflict within themselves. They felt both grief and the desire to dance with joy.

Dismay, disarray arrived at the moment the radio reported Stalin's state: "Cheyne-Stokes breathing . . . urine . . . pulse . . . blood pressure . . ." The deified sovereign suddenly disclosed his weak and senile flesh.

Stalin had died! And in his death was that element of spontaneity infinitely alien to the nature of the Stalinist state.

This spontaneity made the state shudder, as it had shuddered with the shock of June 22, 1941.

Millions clamored to see the body. Not only Moscow but the provinces as well poured in upon the Hall of Columns where he lay in state. The line of trucks stretched outside Moscow for miles and miles. Traffic was blocked as far south as Serpukhov. The ensuing paralysis brought to a halt the traffic between Serpukhov and Tula too.

Millions swarmed on foot toward the center of Moscow. Streams of people, like black, crackling rivers, crashed into each other, rolled up against masonry barriers, writhed and twisted, crushed cars, tore iron gates from their hinges. Thousands died, trampled to death. The coronation day of Nicholas II on Khodynka Field was eclipsed by the death day of the Russian god—the pockmarked shoemaker's son from Gori.

People seemed to march to their deaths in a state of hypnosis, in some kind of mystical Christian-Buddhist acceptance of doom. It was as if Stalin, the great shepherd, had finished off the still unslaughtered sheep, posthumously eliminating the element of chance from his dread over-all plan.

Stalin's comrades-in-arms, assembled in session, read the monstrous communiqués from the Moscow militia, from the morgues, and looked at each other in horror. Their confusion was closely related to the unfamiliar feeling of not being afraid of the great Stalin's implacable fury. The master was dead.

On April 5 Nikolai Andreyevich waked up his wife and exclaimed: "Masha! The doctors are innocent! Masha, they were tortured!"

The state had admitted its awful guilt—it had confessed that "impermissible means of interrogation" had been applied to the accused doctors.

After the first moment of joy, the first moment of bright relief, Nikolai Andreyevich felt unexpected, unfamiliar pangs. He had never felt anything like them before.

He was experiencing a new and strange feeling of guilt for his cowardice, for his readiness to give his consent to obvious falsehood, for the fact that this consent had arisen within him voluntarily, from the very bottom of his heart.

Had he lived right? Had he really been honest, and how did those around him feel about it?

His feeling of anguish and repentance grew stronger.

In the hour when the divine, faultless state had repented of its own crime, Nikolai Andreyevich sensed its mortal, earthly flesh—the state too, like Stalin, had suffered heart tremors, had albumen in its urine.

The divinity, the faultlessness, of the immortal state, it now turned out, had not only crushed the individual human being, but had also defended him, comforted him in his weakness, shielded him and provided justification for his insignificance. The state had taken on its own iron shoulders the entire weight of responsibility; it had freed individual human beings from any qualms of conscience.

But here and now Nikolai Andreyevich suddenly felt as

if he were stark-naked, as if thousands of hostile eyes were gazing upon his naked body.

And the most unpleasant thing about it was that he, too, stood there in the crowd, with everyone else, staring at his own naked body, at his breasts as pendulous as those of a woman, at his wrinkled stomach stretched by overeating, at the fatty, liverish folds of his flanks.

Yes, Stalin, as it turned out, had lapses of the pulse, and the state, as it turned out, had excreted urine, and Nikolai Andreyevich had turned out to be naked beneath his expensive suit.

How unpleasant that self-examination was! The loathsome record was unbelievably repulsive.

Included in it were general sessions of the Learned Council, formal anniversary and holiday assemblies, brief laboratory propaganda meetings, articles, two books, banquets, dinner parties with evil and important people, voting, jokes at dinner, conversations with personnel directors, signatures at the bottom of letters, and appointments with the minister.

And then, too, in the whole scroll of his life there were many other things: things which should have been done but were not done. Letters not written though God commanded that they be written. Silence when God had commanded that a word be said. Telephones on which calls should have been made but weren't. Visits it was a sin not to have paid but which weren't paid. Money unsent. Telegrams unsent. There was much that ought to have been in the scroll of his life that wasn't there.

And for him, standing there naked, it was simply out of place to be proud of the things he had always been proud of: that he had never denounced anyone to the police; that he had refused, when summoned to the Lubyanka, to give compromising information about a colleague who had been arrested; that he had not turned his back on the wife of an exiled friend when he met her on the street but had clasped her hand and asked about the children.

What was there to be proud of in all that?

His entire life had consisted of one long act of submission, without one single refusal to submit, none whatsoever.

Take his relations with Ivan. For three decades Ivan had been shuttled about in prisons and camps. Nikolai Andreyevich, who always took pride in the fact that he had never made a declaration condemning and renouncing Ivan, had never once written to him. When Ivan had once written to Nikolai Andreyevich, Nikolai had asked his aged aunt to reply.

That used to seem natural; now suddenly it was a source of alarm and pangs of conscience.

He remembered a meeting that dealt with the 1937 trials, at which he had voted for the death sentence for Rykov and Bukharin.

For nearly two decades he had not given a thought to such meetings.

When at that time a certain professor in the Mining Institute, whose name Nikolai Andreyevich could not even recall, and the poet Pasternak had refused to vote for the death sentence for Bukharin, it had seemed outlandish and insane. After all, the criminals had confessed at their trials. After all, they had been publicly questioned by an educated, university man: Andrei Yanuaryevich Vyshinsky. After all, there had been no doubt about their guilt, not one shadow of a doubt.

But now Nikolai Andreyevich remembered that there had been doubts. He had only pretended there were none. Because even had he thought Bukharin innocent, he would have had to vote for the death sentence anyway. It was just easier not to doubt if one was going to vote for the death sentence, so he had simply pretended to himself that he had no doubts. He had to vote for the death sentence anyway because he did believe in the great goals of the Lenin-Stalin Party. He did believe that for the first time in history a socialist society without private property had been built, and that socialism required a dictatorship of the state. To doubt Bukharin's guilt, to refuse to vote, would have meant to have doubts about the mighty state, about its great purposes.

But, for that matter, somewhere deep down in his soul he doubted even this holy belief, this faith.

How could it be socialism—out in the Kolyma, in the cannibalism during the time of collectivization, in the deaths of millions of people?

Then something quite different would worm its way into the depths of his consciousness—the realization that the terror was terribly inhuman, that the sufferings of the workers and peasants were indeed very, very great.

Yes, yes, his entire life had been spent in kowtowing, in a great act of submission, in terror of starvation, torture, and Siberian hard labor. There had been, in addition, one particularly low form of fear—the fear of receiving red caviar in place of black caviar. And his youthful dreams in the years of War Communism had, in fact, played into the hands of this low, foul, "caviar" fear too. Anything so as not to be troubled by doubt—vote for and sign anything, everything, without thinking. Yes, yes, it was fear for his own skin, it was cowardice that had nourished his ideological strength.

Suddenly the state had shuddered and muttered that the doctors had been tortured. And tomorrow, perhaps, the state would confess that Bukharin, Zinoviev, Kamenev, Rykov, and Pyatakov had been tortured, that Maxim Gorky had not been murdered by enemies of the people. And the day after tomorrow, perhaps, the government would confess that millions of peasants had been killed off to no good purpose.

And then, it seemed to him, it would ultimately turn out that the state had not after all taken upon itself the guilt for everything; and that Nikolai Andreyevich would have to answer for it.

And there it all was: he had had no doubts; he had voted for everything; he had signed his name to everything. He had learned to pretend to himself so skillfully that no one, not even he himself, had seen that it was pretending. He had actually taken honest pride in his faith and his purity.

The anguished feeling of self-contempt was at moments so great that a bitter, sharp reproach against the state rose within him: why had it confessed? It should have kept silent! The state had no right to confess! Everything should have been left as it was!

Professor Margolin, who declared he was prepared, for the sake of the great cause of internationalism, to put to death not merely the doctor-assassins but his own Jewish children, no doubt really felt that way.

The burden of long years of submissive filth was simply too much for the conscience to bear.

But gradually Nikolai Andreyevich's feeling of depression began to ease. Everything, it would seem, had changed, and yet, apparently, it had not changed.

Work at the Institute had become incomparably easier, more relaxed. This was especially so since Ryskov had been removed as director because his rudeness had aroused anger in high places.

The success of which Nikolai Andreyevich had dreamed had finally arrived—not just in relation to his own institution or within the government apparatus; it was a real, genuine, great success. It made itself felt in all kinds of ways —in articles, in statements by participants in scientific conferences, in the excitement in the eyes of colleagues and laboratory technicians, in the letters he had begun to receive.

Nikolai Andreyevich had been promoted to the Supreme Learned Council; soon afterward, the Presidium of the Academy of Sciences had confirmed his appointment as the scientific head of the Institute.

Nikolai Andreyevich had tried to bring back into the Institute the expelled cosmopolites and idealists, but it turned out he was quite unable to get approval for this from the chief of the personnel department, a very pleasant and attractive, yet terribly stubborn, woman. He had had to content himself with providing nonstaff, free-lance piecework for his former colleagues.

And nowadays when he looked upon Mandelshtam, Nikolai Andreyevich marveled; was it possible that this pitiful, helpless man, delivering a package of translations and annotations to the Institute, had been described abroad only a few years earlier as a very important, perhaps even a great, scientist? Was it possible that Nikolai Andreyevich had once been passionately anxious for his approval?

Previously Mandelshtam had dressed carelessly, but now

he came to the Institute in his best suit. Nikolai Andreyevich had joked about this—and Mandelshtam had replied: "After all, an unemployed actor must always put up a good front."

And right now, in the process of recalling his past life, it seemed to Nikolai Andreyevich strangely bitter and yet sweet to imagine the coming encounter with Ivan. Within the family, the accepted view had been that Ivan was the most promising in brains and talent of all their age group. Nikolai Andreyevich himself had come to accept this opinion. Well, it wasn't that he had accepted it—he hadn't at all. He had submitted to it.

Ivan read math and physics texts with amazing speed, and he mastered them not compliantly but creatively, making them his own in his individual way. From childhood he had revealed a talent for sculpting. He had the ability to reproduce in clay facial expressions, peculiarities of gesture, and, particularly, movements in a very lifelike way. In addition, he developed a fascinated interest in the ancient East. He was an expert in the literature about Parthian manuscripts and monuments.

From early childhood, also, he had revealed a unique combination of personality and character traits.

Once this boy realist had bloodied an opponent in a fight so badly that he was held for two days by the militia.

Yet he was shy, gentle, and sensitive; and in a small den beneath the house he used to have a hospital in which he cared for crippled animals: a dog with one missing paw, a blind cat, a sad jackdaw with one wing.

As a university student Ivan was just as unusual in combining sensitivity, gentleness toward others, kindness, and shyness with a pitiless curtness and brusqueness that forced even those close to him to feel a grudge against him.

Possibly these very traits were what led to Ivan's failure to fulfill the hopes people had had for him. Ivan's life was ruined, and he himself had helped to ruin it.

In the twenties many talented young people could not get into institutions of higher education because of their social origin. The children of members of the nobility, czarist military officers, priests, factory owners, and tradesmen were denied admission.

But Ivan was accepted at the university. His family came from the working intelligentsia. He got through the harsh university purge based on class origin without any difficulty.

And had Ivan been about to begin life over again, the present cruel difficulties connected with point five of the security and personnel questionnaires—in other words nationality, in other words Jewish nationality in particular—would not have concerned him.

Yet, at the same time, as Nikolai Andreyevich saw it, if Ivan were to begin his life all over again in the present era, he would once again fail.

Ivan's failures were not matters of external circumstances. His bitter fate was rooted within him.

In the philosophy discussion group at the university, he had argued bitterly with the teachers of dialectical materialism. They finally shut down the discussion group.

At that point, Ivan spoke out in a lecture hall against dictatorship. He proclaimed freedom a boon as important as life itself, and declared that limitations on freedom cripple people as surely as an ax that cuts off their fingers or their ears, and that the annihilation of freedom is the equivalent of murder. After this speech he was expelled from the university and exiled for three years to Semipalatinsk Province.

Since then thirty years had passed. In all those decades Ivan had been free for not more than one year. The last time Nikolai Andreyevich had seen him was in 1936, not long before he was rearrested; after that he spent nineteen continuous years in camps.

The comrades of his childhood and his student years remembered him for a long time; they would say: "Ivan would have been an academician by now." "Yes, he was a very special person, but, of course, he was unlucky." And certain of them said: "Of course, he is insane."

Anya Zamkovskaya, the love of Ivan's life, had remembered him longer than anyone else.

But time worked its way. And Anya, by now the ailing and gray Anna Vladimirovna, when they met at the theater or at Gaspra in the fall, never asked about Ivan any more.

He had disappeared from people's consciousness, from hot and cold hearts; his existence was clandestine; and as the years passed, those who had known him recalled him to mind with ever greater difficulty.

Time worked its way, without haste, conscientiously. The individual was first stricken from the scene of actual day-to-day life and migrated into people's memory; then he lost his place in their memory as well and disappeared into the subconscious; finally, he put in an appearance on the surface only very rarely, and, when he did, caused fright by his sudden momentary presence.

And time continued to work its infinitely simple earthy way, and Ivan had already made one whole big further step from the deep dark cellar of his friends' subconscious into permanent residence in nonbeing, into eternal oblivion.

But then came the new post-Stalin period, and fate decreed that Ivan should walk once again in that life which had lost both the thought of him and his visual image.

4

Ivan Grigoryevich did not arrive at Nikolai Andreyevich's apartment until evening.

In the excitement of their reunion, apologies and regrets that the lavish luncheon had been kept waiting on the table overlong mingled with exclamations over gray hair and wrinkles, and remarks about how life had passed. And, as Nikolai Andreyevich described the death of their only son, as they once again relived it, copious tears flowed from his eyes—like a flood unleashed by a thunderstorm, boiling and bubbling in a dry old clay ravine—and Mariya Pavlovna also wept.

The swarthy, wrinkled face, and the padded cotton jacket, and the awkward government-issue soldier's shoes of the man from the world of the camps were out of tune with Nikolai Andreyevich's world of parquet floors, glass-enclosed bookcases, paintings, and chandeliers.

Suppressing his excitement and gazing on his cousin with eyes dimmed by his own tears, Ivan Grigoryevich said:

"Nikolai, first I want to say that I have no requests to

make of you—not about getting permission to live in Moscow, nor money, nor anything else. And, incidentally, I have already visited a bath, and I have no lice."

Nikolai Andreyevich, wiping away his tears, began to laugh: "Gray-headed and wrinkled, but still just the same —our Vanya!"

He made a circle in the air and then pierced this imaginary circle with his finger.

"Totally insufferable, as direct and straight as an arrow, and along with all that—and only the good Lord knows how it can be—kind and good."

Mariya Pavlovna exchanged looks with Nikolai Andreyevich. That very morning she had attempted to convince her husband that it would be better for Ivan Grigoryevich to go to a public bath rather than to use their bathroom; he simply could not wash up the way he had to in a home bathtub: yes, and after Ivan had washed himself in their bathtub, it would never be clean again, even with acid and lye.

As the conversation progressed, even in its seemingly empty routine there was much more than just talk—smiles, glances, gestures, coughs, all of which helped to disclose, to explain, and to foster understanding among them all over again.

Most of all, Nikolai Andreyevich wanted to talk about himself—far more than to talk about their childhood, or to enumerate all their kinfolk who had died, more, too, than to question Ivan. But since he was well mannered—since, in other words, he was able to do and say what he didn't want to—he said: "We should have gone to the country house where there are no phones, and where I could listen to you for a week, or a month, or two."

Ivan Grigoryevich pictured to himself how, reclining in an armchair, and sipping a glass of wine, he would begin talking of people who had gone into eternal darkness. The fate of many of them seemed so poignantly sad that to speak of them in even the most tender, quiet, kind words would have been like touching a heart torn open with a rough and insensitive hand. It was really quite impossible to speak of them at all.

So, nodding his head, he said: "Yes, yes, the tale of a thousand and one arctic nights."

Ivan Grigoryevich was fascinated. Which was the real Kolya—the one who thirty years before had gone about in a worn sateen shirt, with a book in English under his arm, jolly, quick-witted, and obliging; or this new-found Kolya sitting in front of him, with big soft cheeks and a waxen bald pate?

All his life Ivan had been strong. People had always turned to him for explanations and reassurance. On occasion even the thieves in "India," the notorious camp for incorrigible criminals, had asked his advice. Once he had succeeded in stopping a knife battle between members of the Russian thieves' group, the *"blatnye,"* as they were called, and the "bitches," which was camp jargon for those criminals who had gone over to work for the camp administration as trusties. All kinds of people had respected him—engineers accused of "wrecking"; a torn and tattered czarist officer; a lieutenant colonel from Denikin's armies; a master woodsman with a bow saw; a Minsk gynecologist accused of Jewish bourgeois nationalism; a Crimean Tatar who kept muttering that his people had been driven into the taiga from the shores of the Black Sea; and a collective farmer who had stolen a bag of potatoes from the collective farm, hoping that when he got out of camp he would be able to get a six-month city passport on the strength of his camp-release documents and not have to return to the collective farm.

But on this particular day what Ivan Grigoryevich really longed for was for someone else's good strong arms to lift his burden from his shoulders. And he knew that there was only one force in the world before which it was wonderful and comforting to feel oneself small and weak—one's mother. But his mother had long since gone, and there was no one to lift his burden from him.

Meanwhile a strange feeling arose in Nikolai Andreyevich despite himself.

While waiting for Ivan, Nikolai Andreyevich, deeply moved, had thought how totally honest he would be with him, as he had been with no one else in his whole life. He would confess to Ivan all his pangs of conscience, set forth abjectly all his vile and bitter weakness.

So Vanya would pass judgment on him if he could. Understand him if he could and forgive him. And if he couldn't—all right, so be it. He was nervous and excited, and tears dimmed his eyes as he repeated to himself several times the Nekrasov verses:

> The son knelt down before the father,
> And washed the old man's feet. . . .

He wanted to convince his cousin: "Vanya, Vanyechka, it sounds crazy, wild, but I envy you. I envy you because in your terrible camps you did not have to sign vile letters, nor vote for the death of innocent men, nor make foul speeches."

But now, with Ivan there in front of him, he experienced a sudden turnabout of feeling. This man in a padded jacket, in soldier's shoes, his face eaten away by the cold of Siberia and the foul air of overcrowded camp barracks, struck him as alien, spiteful, hostile.

He had had exactly this same feeling during trips abroad. He had found it unthinkable, impossible, to discuss his doubts with carefully groomed foreigners or to share the gall of what he had seen and suffered. And so with them he had talked only of the main, the unquestionable thing—the historical achievements of the Soviet state. He had erected defenses against them for the Motherland.

But could he ever have imagined that Ivan, too, could arouse such feelings in him? How could it have happened —and yet it had!

Ivan, he now felt, had come here purposely to reduce his whole life to nothing. Ivan intended to humiliate him, to talk down to him.

He burned with the desire to force Ivan to understand, to make quite clear to him that everything was different now, on a new footing, that all the old values had been wiped out, and that Ivan himself was a failure, that his unhappy fate was not accidental, not just bad luck. This gray-haired, ill-starred student, what had he ever accomplished and what was there left for him in life anyway?

And just because Nikolai Andreyevich so burned with the desire to say all this to Ivan, he said something quite the contrary:

"How wonderfully it has all worked out! For the most part, Vanya, we are equals, you and I. Even though there will be times when you feel you have lost whole decades, that you've spent your life for nothing at all, particularly when you run into people who have put in all those years writing books and all the rest of it, instead of cutting wood in the forests or digging ditches in camps, please realize that you must not give it a thought. Essentially, Vanyechka, you are the equal of those who are moving science forward, who have been successful in their lives and work."

He felt his voice trembling with emotion and his heart fluttering deliciously as he spoke. He noted embarrassment on Ivan's face and tears in Mariya Pavlovna's eyes. After all, he loved Ivan. All his life he had loved him. And Mariya Pavlovna felt her husband's greatness of heart more deeply than ever before as he sat there trying to buck up the unfortunate Ivan. She, at any rate, knew who was the conqueror and who the conquered.

It was really quite strange to think that not even when the ZIS limousine was taking Nikolai Andreyevich to Vnukovo Airport for his flight to India, where he was to introduce a delegation of Soviet scientists to Prime Minister Nehru, had she felt so fully her triumph in life. This was something quite special—all bound up with her tears for her dead son, with pity and love for that gray-haired man in his crude shoes.

"Vanya," she said, "I have put together a complete wardrobe for you. You are the same height as Kolya."

This was hardly the time for Mariya Pavlovna to bring up the subject of old suits, and Nikolai Andreyevich said: "Good Lord, why do we have to talk about such nonsense as that? Of course, Vanya, with all my heart . . . whatever I have."

"It's not a matter of heart," said Ivan Grigoryevich. "It's just that you are three times bigger around the waist than I."

Mariya Pavlovna was transfixed by Ivan's attentive and rather compassionate glance. It seemed to her that her husband's unassuming modesty had served only to encourage Vanya to keep on clinging stubbornly to his old condescending attitude toward Nikolai Andreyevich.

Ivan Grigoryevich downed some vodka and his face flushed. He asked about old acquaintances.

Most of these former friends Nikolai Andreyevich had not seen for whole decades. Many were dead. And everything they used to have in common—interests, work, affairs—was gone. Ways had parted. Even his regret and sadness for those who had disappeared into nothingness in the purges—"without the right of correspondence" and without return—had vanished into thin air. Nikolai Andreyevich did not want to recall them—just as a person might be reluctant to approach a solitary, dried-out, bare tree trunk around which lay nothing but dusty, dead earth.

Nikolai Andreyevich wanted to talk about people Ivan had never known, for the events of his own life were bound up with them. Telling about them was his way of approaching his main subject—his own story.

Yes, and it was precisely now, in such moments as these, that it was utterly essential for him to rid himself of, to repress in himself, that ancient worm of the intellectual, his bad conscience, his sense of the illegitimacy of the miraculous thing that had happened to him. He didn't want to confess and repent. He wanted to justify and brag.

And so he began to talk about all those people who had despised him, though without malice, and who had failed to understand or appreciate him—those people whom today he was so generously willing to help.

"Kolyenka," Mariya Pavlovna suddenly blurted out.

"You must tell him about Anya Zamkovskaya."

Husband and wife immediately sensed Ivan Grigoryevich's excitement.

Nikolai Andreyevich asked: "Did she write you?"

"My last letter from her was eighteen years ago."

"Yes, yes, she is married. Her husband is a physical chemist, you know, engaged in all that nuclear business. They live in Leningrad—can you imagine it?—in the very same apartment where she used to live with her family. We usually run into her on vacation, in the fall. She always used to ask about you, but since the war, to tell the truth, she has stopped."

Ivan Grigoryevich coughed and said hoarsely: "I thought she must have died; she stopped writing."

"Oh, yes, and then about Mandelshtam," said Nikolai Andreyevich. "Do you remember old man Zaozersky? Mandelshtam was his favorite student. Zaozersky crashed in 1937. The man traveled abroad, widely in fact, and he met freely with émigrés and defectors—Ipatyev and Chichibanin. . . . Yes, and here's what happened to Mandelshtam. At one point he enjoyed instant success, but I have already told you the upshot of that, how he was proclaimed a 'homeless cosmopolite' and all the rest. What with Zaozersky's carelessness, he was really up to his neck in his European and American scientific connections."

Nikolai Andreyevich believed he was saying these things not for his own sake but to instruct Ivan—after all, Ivan must not be allowed to hang onto his naïve ideas: he needed to be brought up to date. And at this very moment there flashed through his mind: "My Lord, how ingrained in me are false humility and hypocrisy!"

He looked at Ivan's relaxed brown hands and began to explain:

"I know this terminology is very strange to you—'cosmopolitanism,' 'bourgeois nationalism,' 'point five in questionnaires.' Cosmopolitanism is virtually the same as alleged participation in a monarchist plot at the time of the First Congress of the Comintern. But then, come to think of it, you saw them all in camp; those who replaced the first batch, and those who replaced them, and so on and so forth, and they all became your bunkmates. But, as I see it, that sort of thing is no longer a danger; the process of switch-about has been completed. During these decades what was called 'national in form' has very simply and majestically been transformed in our life into 'national in content.' But many people do not want to accept this simple fact. For, after all, if a person has been pushed out and cast aside, he hardly wants to regard it as a consequence of the operation of an historical law; instead, he sees it only as an inept mistake. But the fact remains. Our scientists, our technologists, created Soviet Russian airplanes, Russian uranium piles, and electronic computers; and political sovereignty must correspond to this scientific sovereignty—that which is Russian has been transmuted into actual content, into a basis, a foundation."

He kept saying how much he hated the organizers of pogroms. And yet, at the same time, he could see that Mandelshtam and Khavkin, although unquestionably gifted and talented, had been blind. To them it seemed that everything that had happened was Judophobia and nothing but.

In the same way, men like Pyzhov and Rodionov also failed to understand that what had happened to them and others was not merely a matter of harshness and intolerance on Lysenko's part, but a matter of *national* science, which the new people affirmed.

Ivan Grigoryevich gazed at him attentively, and within Nikolai Andreyevich's heart an alarm rustled—the same kind of alarm he used to experience in childhood when he felt his mother's sad eyes upon him and understood, though unclearly, that what he was doing was wrong, that what he was saying was wrong too. And, wishing to put this vague feeling to rest, he began to deliver particularly emphatic and outspoken judgments.

"I went through trials and tribulations," said Nikolai Andreyevich sadly, sincerely. "I survived a hard and difficult time! Of course, I did not ring out like Herzen's bell. I did not expose Beriya or Stalin's mistakes. But it is silly even to talk of something like that."

Ivan Grigoryevich's head drooped, and it was hard to know whether he was dozing, daydreaming, or pondering Nikolai Andreyevich's words. His hands rested quietly and his head seemed to sink into his shoulders. And that was just how he had been sitting the day before, listening to the men traveling in his compartment.

Nikolai Andreyevich said: "Things went badly for me under Yagoda and Yezhov, and now when Beriya, Abakumov, Ryumin, Merkulov, and Kobulov are all gone, I have at last gotten on my feet. I sleep peacefully and do not expect night visitors. Yes, and in that I am not alone. And involuntarily one thinks it was not in vain that we suffered through all that cruel time. A new life was born, and it is within everyone's capacity to participate in it."

"Kolya, Kolya," said Ivan Grigoryevich softly.

His words angered Mariya Pavlovna. She and her husband had both noticed the gloom and compassion on their guest's face.

Reproachfully she said to her husband: "Why are you

afraid to say that Mandelshtam and Pyzhov are selfish egotists? And why pretend to be sorry that life put them in their place? It certainly did—thanks be!"

She was reproaching her husband, but her reproach was actually directed at their guest. And as a result, worried about her sharp words, she immediately said: "I am going to go and make the bed. Vanya is very tired. We ought to have kept that in mind."

And Ivan Grigoryevich, already realizing that his visit to his cousin had brought him no relief but had merely added to his burden, asked grimly: "Tell me now, did you sign that letter condemning the doctor-assassins? I heard about it in camp from people who were arrested."

"Our dear, dear eccentric!" said Nikolai Andreyevich, and then he faltered and fell silent.

He felt a cold pang of pain inside himself and, at the same time, he began to sweat and his cheeks grew flushed. He finally said: "My dear friend, my dear friend, we, too, had a hard time in our life—it wasn't just you out there in the camps!"

"Good Lord!" Ivan Grigoryevich said hurriedly. "I am not your judge, nor anybody's judge. What kind of a judge can I be? No, no!"

"No, no, not that," said Nikolai Andreyevich. "What I want to say is how important it is, in the midst of all the smoke and dust, not to be blind—to see the greatness of our road, for if one becomes blind, one can go insane."

Ivan Grigoryevich declared guiltily: "Yes, you see my bad luck is that I seem to mistake vision for blindness."

"Where will we put Vanya?" Mariya Pavlovna asked. "Where is he going to be most comfortable?"

Ivan Grigoryevich said: "Oh, no, no, thank you. I really can't spend the night here."

"Why not? Where else but? Masha, let's simply tie him down. . . ." said Nikolai Andreyevich jokingly.

But Ivan Grigoryevich blurted out: "Oh, no, please, I don't want to be tied down. . . ."

And then he caught himself. Nikolai Andreyevich had fallen silent and was frowning.

"Please forgive me. I wasn't really thinking of what I was saying. I didn't mean it that way. It was something quite different," said Ivan Grigoryevich.

"Here's what, Vanya . . ." said Nikolai Andreyevich, and then he fell silent once more.

After Ivan Grigoryevich had gone, Mariya Pavlovna looked at the table, covered with hors d'oeuvres, and at the chairs that had been pushed back from the table.

"We received him like a king," she said. "We did not entertain the President of the Academy of Sciences and his family any more royally."

Truth to tell, Mariya Pavlovna had on this occasion actually prepared a luncheon with the great bounty and generosity characteristic of lavish natures. And that is something that happens only rarely with stingy people.

Nikolai Andreyevich went up to the table.

"Yes, indeed, if a man is insane, then he's insane for his whole life."

She put her palms on his temples and, kissing his forehead, declared: "Please don't be in a bad mood, please, my incorrigible idealist!"

5

Ivan Grigoryevich woke up as dawn approached. He was lying on the shelf-bunk of a "hard"-class railway coach, listening to the clicking of the train wheels. He opened his eyes just a bit and stared out the window into the gray half-light outside.

Several times in his thirty years of imprisonment he had had vivid dreams of childhood scenes. There was one occasion when he had dreamed of a tiny inlet of the sea, with still water and tiny stones covering the bottom. Several small crabs had scampered off sideways and hidden in the reeds. He had walked slowly among the rounded pebbles, lazily feeling the tender underwater grass on his feet. And then dozens of elongated drops of quicksilver—mackerel minnows—had flashed past and scattered. The sun lit up the green pools of underwater weeds. And the illusion clung that the little inlet was filled not with water but with light.

He had had this dream in a prisoner-transport freight car. A quarter-century had passed since that day. Yet he could still recall the terrible pain that struck him when he awoke to see the gray light of winter and the gray faces of the other prisoners, when he heard outside the car the crunching of jackboots in the snow, and the dull knocking of the search mallets of the guards along the bottom of the car, testing for sawed boards.

Sometimes in such dreams he saw his childhood home standing high above the sea, the branches of their ancient cherry tree bending over the roof, and their well. . . .

He had developed his memory to the point of anguishing sharpness, and he could recover the gleam of the thick magnolia leaf, the flat stone in the midst of the stream. . . . He could recapture the silence and the coolness of the rooms with white plaster walls, the design of the tablecloth. He could remember reading, with legs drawn up beneath him on the couch—and the pleasant coolness of the oil-cloth on the divan on hot summer days. He sometimes tried to recall his mother's face, and at such moments his heart ached, and tears would appear in his squinched-up eyes, just as in childhood when he tried to look at the sun.

He easily recalled the mountains in full detail—it was like leafing through a well-worn book that opened on its own to the correct page. Scrambling through blackberry clumps, through brush, skidding on the flinty, yellowish-gray, crackling earth, he climbed up to the watershed, and, looking back at the sea, entered the cool twilight of the forest. . . . On thick branches, the powerful oaks lifted airily up to the heavens their hillocks of intricate leaves, and moist stillness hovered all around.

In the mid-nineteenth century the places along that coast had been settled by Circassians.

An old Greek, the gardener Methodius, had himself as a

boy seen the thickly settled Circassian auls and their orchards.

After the Russian conquest of the shoreline, the Circassians departed, and life had died out up in the coastal mountains. Among the oaks there still grew in some places bent-over plum trees which had gone wild, but the short-lived pear trees, cherry trees, peach trees, and apricots had all disappeared.

In the forest lay gloomy, sooty stones, remnants of ruined hearths; in abandoned cemeteries the gravestones had darkened and sunk halfway into the ground.

Everything lifeless—stones, iron, and all the rest—had over the years been swallowed up by the earth, had dissolved into it; but the green life had, in contrast, sprung from the earth with ever-renewed vitality. The silence hovering over the cold hearths seemed painful to the boy. And on returning home, he was overjoyed to smell the odor of smoke from their kitchen, to hear the dogs barking, the hens cackling. Once he went up to his mother, who was sitting beside a table, reading a book, and embraced her, pressing his head against her knees.

"Are you ill?" she asked.

"No, I am not ill, I am just happy," he murmured, kissing his mother's dress, and then he wept.

He was quite unable to explain how he felt to his mother. He had the feeling that in the darkness of the forest someone was moaning, seeking the people who had gone, looking out from behind trees, trying to hear the voices of Circassian shepherds, the weeping of Circassian infants, and sniffing the air for the odor of smoke and hot unleavened bread.

Somehow he felt not only joy but shame at the loveliness

of his own home when he returned from the woods.

But he failed to make this clear to his mother when he tried to explain. She said to him: "You're my foolish little darling. How hard it will be for you to go through life with such a tender, easily wounded heart!"

After dinner his father, exchanging glances with his mother, said to him: "Vanya, I am certain you know our Sochi used to be called Post Dakhovsky and that the villages in our mountains were called First Regiment and Second Regiment."

"Yes, I know," he said and sniffed out of pique.

"They were the camps of Russian military units. The soldiers marched with axes and spades as well as guns, and they cut roads through the forests in which wild, cruel mountaineers lived."

His father scratched the beard under his chin, and added: "Forgive my pomposity—but they cut a roadway for Russia! That is why we were able to make our homes here. I helped organize the schools, and, let's say, Yakov Yakovlevich planted vineyards and orchards, and others built hospitals and made roads. Progress demands sacrifices, and there is no use crying over the inevitable. Do you understand why I am saying all this?"

"I understand," replied Vanya. "But there were orchards here before we came that have now gone wild."

"Yes, my friend, yes," said his father. "When they chop down the forest, the chips will fly! And, for that matter, the Circassians were not driven out of here. They left for Turkey of their own free will. They could have remained and profited from Russian culture. In Turkey they became paupers and many died."

Yes, in his dreams Ivan recalled everything he had experienced—he dreamed of his home, and he heard familiar voices, and he heard the barking of their old watchdog as he rose to greet him with eyes reddened by senile tears.

And then he awakened to the roar of the taiga-ocean over which a winter blizzard was raging.

So now his days of life in freedom had come, and all the time he had kept waiting, hoping, for the return of something good, something young.

On the morning after seeing Nikolai Andreyevich he awakened there in the "hard"-class coach with a feeling of desperate loneliness. His encounter with his cousin the day before had filled his cup with gall. And Moscow itself had choked and oppressed him. The hugeness of the skyscrapers, the heavy auto traffic, the traffic lights, the crowds of pedestrians on the sidewalks, all seemed hostile and strange to him. The city seemed an enormous mechanism trained to stop on the red light and start moving again on the green. Russia had seen much in the course of its thousand years of history. In the Soviet years the country had seen world-shaking military victories, vast construction projects, new cities, dams blocking the Dnieper and the Volga, a canal uniting seas, the power of tractors, and skyscrapers. There was just one thing that Russia had not seen in all its thousand years—freedom.

During his day in Moscow he had traveled in a trolley-bus through the new southwest district of the city. In the midst of rural mud, of village ponds not yet dried up, had risen great eight- and ten-story buildings. The village huts, vegetable gardens, little old sheds, had come to their end, crushed by the enormous advance of stone and asphalt.

In the chaos, in the roar of the five-ton trucks, the outlines of the future streets of Moscow could be imagined.

Ivan Grigoryevich wandered about this city rising without benefit of sidewalks and pavements. People made their way to their homes along paths and trails winding through piles of trash. Everywhere on the buildings hung the same signs: "Meat," "Barber Shop." In the twilight the vertical signs of "Meat" burned like red fire, and "Barber Shop" shone with a penetrating green.

These signs, which arrived with the very first residents, seemed somehow to disclose, to uncover, the fleshly essence of the human being.

Meat, meat! The human being could not get along without meat. There were no libraries, no theaters, no cinemas, no tailor shops, not even any hospitals, pharmacies, schools. But right from the start, in the midst of all the masonry work, a red light gleamed out: "Meat, meat." And then came the emerald of the barber shop signs. The human being eats meat and grows wool.

At night, after seeing his cousin, Ivan Grigoryevich had gone to the station and found that the last train for Leningrad left at 2 A.M. He brought himself a ticket and went to get his things from the checkroom.

On entering the cold, empty car he was astonished at his feeling of immediate relaxation.

After pulling out of the station and leaving the city, the train passed through the outskirts of Moscow. Through the window dark autumn copses and glades flashed by. Ivan Grigoryevich felt easier in his heart because he was slipping away from the Moscow leviathan of electricity, masonry, and automobiles, and was no longer listening to his cousin's recital of the rationality of the historical process which had cleared a path for him. On the polished surface of the shelf-bunk, as in water, was reflected the gleam of the conductor's flashlight.

"Hey there, daddy! What about your ticket?"

"I've already shown it."

Just think, for years he had pictured to himself the day when he would return to freedom and would see his cousin again, the only person left in the whole world who had known his childhood, his mother, his father.

Now he had seen him, and in the morning he had awakened with a sense of overwhelming and unbearable loneliness.

He was going to the city where he had spent years as a university student, where the love of his life still lived.

Many years before, when she had stopped writing, he had mourned her—he had had no doubt at all that death alone could break off their correspondence. And yet she had been alive. She had been alive all this time.

6

Ivan Grigoryevich stayed in Leningrad three days. He visited the Okhta district, the Polytechnical Institute, and went to the university twice. He sought out the remembered residences of friends of his student days. Sometimes he could not find the streets; sometimes the buildings he was looking for had been demolished in the siege; then again, even when he found an apartment house still standing, there would be no trace of anyone there whom he had known.

Walking through familiar places he might find himself in a state of completely calm absent-mindedness—absorbed in memories of people and conversations in camp. Then, too, he might come to a stop before a familiar building or crossing, immersed in a recollection from the years of his youth.

He went through the Hermitage—to find that it left him cold and indifferent. It was unbearable to think that those paintings had remained as beautiful as ever during the years in camp which had transformed him into a prematurely old man. Why hadn't the faces of the madonnas grown old too, and why hadn't their eyes been blinded with tears? Was not their immortality their failure rather than their strength? Did not their changelessness reveal a betrayal by art of the humanity which had created it?

On one particular occasion the intensity of sudden recollection was terribly poignant—though the incident he remembered seemed happenstance and insignificant: he had helped an elderly crippled woman by carrying her basket up to the fourth floor and then dashed down the dark stairwell and emerged into the daylight and shouted with joy—at spring, at the puddles, at the March sun.

He approached the apartment house where Anya Zamkovskaya, his former fiancée, lived. But it seemed unthinkable to go in. How often he had pictured it to himself! Its tall windows, the granite facing of the walls, the marble of the steps pallid in the half-light of the staircase, the metal lacework surrounding the elevator shaft. He used to walk Anya home after their evening strolls and then stand beneath her window, waiting until she lit her light. And she had once told him: "Even if you were to go to war and return a blind cripple without arms or legs, I would be happy in your love!"

Now, thirty years later, he could see flowers up there on the sill of her half-opened window. He stood for a little while near her entry and then went his way. His heart did not skip a beat. When he was behind barbed wire thousands of miles away, this woman, whom he had believed dead, had been nearer his heart than when he stood beneath her window today.

The city was familiar yet unfamiliar. Much of it seemed as unchanged as if he had been absent for only a few hours.

There was much—buildings and whole streets—that was completely new. And much had disappeared without a trace.

And Ivan Grigoryevich failed to understand that it was not merely a matter of the city's having changed but that he himself had changed too: his interests and his searching gaze.

Now he could see elements in the city he had never been conscious of before. It was as if he had been given new eyes. Ranged before him now were secondhand clothing dealers, militia stations, passport registration desks, beer halls and greasy-spoon joints, employment agencies, job-announcement boards, hospitals, and overnight accommodations for transients in the railroad stations.

And the city he used to know—the city of theater posters, symphony orchestras, secondhand bookstores, stadiums, and university lecture halls—had disappeared into the fourth dimension.

After all, for a chronic invalid, the only things in a city are pharmacies, hospitals, clinics, and doctors' offices. For drunkards, a city consists of bars and bottles. For lovers, it consists of the hands on the city clocks which point to the time of the rendezvous, park benches, and two-kopeck coins for pay telephones.

There had been a time when familiar faces were everywhere on these same streets, when at night lights shone everywhere from the windows of people he knew. And now? In his mind's eye familiar faces were all about him, smiling at him from camp cots, whispering with pale lips: "Greetings, Ivan Grigoryevich!"

Once in this city he had known the faces of salesclerks in food stores and bookstores, newspaper and cigarette vendors in kiosks.

Once at Vorkuta a certain jailer had come up to him and said: "I know you. You were once in the Omsk Transit Prison."

Today Ivan Grigoryevich found no familiar faces in the Leningrad crowds. Beyond that, the crowds themselves seemed strange, different. The faces of Leningrad had changed.

Visible and invisible ties to the past had been broken—by time, by the mass deportations after Kirov, by the storms, snows, and dust of Kazakhstan, by the famine of the wartime blockade. They no longer existed. And here stood Ivan Grigoryevich, a stranger and alone.

The migrations of millions had switched things all about; blue-eyed people with high cheekbones had swarmed into Leningrad from the small towns and the countryside; in camp barracks, on the other hand, Ivan Grigoryevich had often met old-time native St. Petersburgers who habitually burred their "r's."

The Nevsky Prospekt and Russia's log-cabin backwoods crudity had met and mingled, not only in buses and apartments, but on the pages of books and magazines and in the conference halls of scientific institutes.

Ivan Grigoryevich could sense here, far away from camp, the spirit of camp. Peering into the windows of Leningrad militia stations, listening across the lavishly spread table to his cousin's speeches, looking at the sign indicating the passport section at police headquarters, Ivan Grigoryevich thought to himself that barbed wire was no longer necessary, that life outside the barbed wire had been assimilated in its inner essence into life in camp.

The enormous pot boiled and bubbled and sporadically crackled, all wreathed in smoke, flame, and steam; and many a man indeed cherished the illusion that he and he alone had grasped the law of the great pot's boiling, that he alone knew the secret of how the stew had been cooked and who was going to eat it.

And then came the day when Ivan Grigoryevich, wearing his government-issue clodhoppers, stood once again beside the Neva, before the divinely barefoot horseman crowned with a laurel wreath. He had passed this way as a youth thirty years before, and then, too, the bronze Peter the Great was full of power. Here, at last, Ivan Grigoryevich had encountered an acquaintance.

And to Ivan Grigoryevich it seemed as if neither thirty years before nor one hundred and thirty years before, when Pushkin had brought his hero to this square, had the divine Peter been so mighty as today. There was no power in the world so immense as that which he had gathered unto himself and expressed—the majestic power of the divine state. It had grown and grown. It had come to reign over fields and factories, over the writing desks of poets and scientists, over the construction sites of dams and canals, over stone quarries, timber forests, sawmills. And it had the capacity in all its mighty power to establish its dominion not only over an area which was vast in its physical, geographical expanses, but also over the innermost, deepest heart of each hypnotized human being who was willing to offer up to it as a gift, in sacrifice, his freedom, and even his very wish for freedom.

"Saint Petersburg, Sanitary Pass, Saint Petersburg, Sanitary Pass." Ivan Grigoryevich kept repeating to himself over and over again a nonsense phrase that had for some reason popped into his mind and that somehow seemed to him to express a tie between the great bronze horseman and himself, the camp bum.

Ivan Grigoryevich spent his nights at the railway station in the room for passengers in transit. He was allowing himself no more than a ruble and a half or two rubles a day for living expenses, and he was not in any rush to leave Leningrad.

On his third day he encountered an acquaintance whom he had often remembered in camp.

Ivan Grigoryevich in no way resembled the third-year university student he had been before his first arrest. And the acquaintance he ran into, Vitaly Antonovich Pinegin, dressed in a dignified gray raincoat and felt hat, was certainly nothing like the youth who had been dressed in a worn student's tunic thirty years before. Yet they recognized each other instantly.

Pinegin stood dumfounded. And it was Ivan Grigoryevich who spoke:

"I suppose you thought I was dead."

Pinegin spread out his hands. "Well I did hear . . . Someone did say ten years ago that . . ."

With bright and lively eyes he peered into the depths of the eyes of Ivan Grigoryevich.

"Don't worry," said Ivan Grigoryevich. "I have not been resurrected from the dead—nor, which would be worse, am I a fugitive. Like you, I, too, have a passport and all the rest."

Pinegin was irritated.

"When I run into an old friend, I am not in the habit of making inquiries about his passport."

He had reached the top, but in his heart he had remained a nice fellow.

And no matter what he went on talking about—his sons, or how much Ivan Grigoryevich had changed, or the like—

his eyes kept an eager and almost spellbound watch over Ivan Grigoryevich.

"Yes, so that's the way it is in a nutshell," Pinegin said. "What else is there to tell you?"

Ivan Grigoryevich kept his thought to himself: "You would do well to speak of something else!"

For a fleeting moment Pinegin froze, almost as if he had sensed the unspoken comment.

"I know nothing at all about you," said Pinegin.

Once again there was a second of expectancy, as if Ivan Grigoryevich might reply: "But, after all, when you found it appropriate, you managed to tell nearly as much about me as I knew myself."

Ivan kept silent and merely spread his hands.

Suddenly Pinegin realized that Ivan Grigoryevich knew nothing. It had been just his nerves! Why the devil had he chosen today to send his car in for a checkup? It was not so very long ago, he recalled, that he had thought about Ivan and wondered what would happen if at this late date one of his relatives were to set about trying to get him rehabilitated posthumously. And here, out of a clear sky, was Ivan himself. Transferred from the dead souls to the living! He had served thirty years and no doubt he had in his pocket a piece of paper saying: "Released for lack of evidence."

Once more he stared into Ivan Grigoryevich's eyes and got his final reassurance that Ivan knew nothing, nothing at all. He was immediately ashamed of his heart tremors, and his cold sweat, and of having been on the point of starting to whimper and whine.

And his feeling of certainty that Ivan would not, after all, spit in his face, would make no demands upon him, filled

Pinegin with elation. And out of some unimaginable generosity he even offered: "Listen here, Ivan, just between us, as friends, in the way of working people, for my father after all was a blacksmith—maybe you need money? Believe me, please, this is just out of friendship, with all my heart."

With alert and sad curiosity Ivan Grigoryevich looked unreproachfully into Pinegin's eyes. And Pinegin for one second only, just one brief second or perhaps two, felt he would gladly sacrifice his country house, his government decorations and honors, his authority and his power, his strength, his beautiful wife, his successful sons engaged in studying the nucleus of the atom—that he would give up every last bit of it, just so as not to feel those eyes resting upon him.

"Well, good luck, Pinegin," said Ivan Grigoryevich, and he went off in the direction of the railway station.

7

Who was guilty and who is going to answer for it?

We have to ponder this question. We must not be too hasty with our answer.

Here they are, the denunciations. There are faked conclusions in testimony by technical specialists—engineers, literary critics, etc. There are speeches denouncing and exposing enemies of the people. And there are the heart-to-heart talks and confessions to a friend rearranged and worked over until they turn into the denunciations and "reports" of the police stoolies and informers.

The denunciations were the prelude to a warrant for arrest, followed by an interrogation, which found its subsequent expression in a sentence. Presumably, these megatons of denunciatory falsehood determined who would be classified as kulaks and liquidated, who would be deprived of their civil rights, of their passports, exiled, shot.

At one end of this chain two people drank tea and talked across a table. Then afterward, in cozy lamplight, an intelligently phrased report was composed. Or perhaps it was merely a speech delivered by a Party activist at a collective farm assembly. And at the other end of the chain were crazed eyes; smashed kidneys; a skull pierced by a bullet; rotting, infected, gangrenous toes; and scurvy-racked corpses in log-cabin, dugout morgues.

In the beginning was the word: truly, truly.

So what shall be done with the police-informer murderers?

Here, for example, is a man who has returned from twenty years in camp with shaking hands, with the sunken eyes of a martyr: this is Judas the First.

Among his friends the word is whispered about. During his interrogation he behaved badly. Certain of his acquaintances have even stopped greeting him on the street. The wiser among them are polite when they happen to meet but do not invite him to their homes. Those wiser still, more generous and profound of heart, invite him to their homes, but keep their hearts closed to him.

They, to be sure, all have country homes, savings account books, decorations and orders, automobiles. Of course, he is thin and they are fat, but it is perfectly true that they did not behave badly under interrogation. Properly speaking, they couldn't have, because no one interrogated them. They were lucky and no one arrested them. Now where precisely lies the genuine spiritual superiority of these fat people to the thin man? Was it luck or some law that determined their separate fates?

He was an ordinary person. He used to drink tea, eat scrambled eggs, and loved to chat with his friends about books he had read. He used to go to the Moscow Art Theater.

On occasion he was kind and generous. True, he was

high-strung and nervous, and he had no self-assurance.

They really put the heat on him too. They shouted at him, beat him, kept him from sleeping, and gave him nothing to drink while feeding him salt herring and threatening him with death. And yet he did an awful crime—he slandered an innocent person. True, the person slandered was not arrested, while he, forced into slander, served out twenty years of hard labor in camp, though innocent of the charges against him. He returned just barely alive, broken, a pauper, on his last legs. But he had, to be sure, slandered another person. . . .

Let us not be hasty. Let us think seriously about this informer.

Here is Judas Number Two.

This one never spent a day in prison. He had the reputation of being bright and silver-tongued. But then people returned from camp all but dead and reported that he was a police informer. He helped to destroy many people. For years he had heart-to-heart talks with his friends and then wrote out reports on them and turned them in to his chiefs. His testimony was not forced from him by torture. He himself took the initiative and cleverly led those he was with to speak about dangerous subjects. Two of those whom he slandered did not return. One was shot by sentence of the Military Collegium. Those who did return came home with illnesses and ailments that left them invalids for the rest of their lives.

The informer in the meantime got himself a paunch, and became famous as a gourmet and a connoisseur of Georgian wines. He worked in the field of the fine arts, and was, among other things, a collector of rare editions of old poetry.

But let us not be overhasty here either. Let us ponder carefully before handing down a verdict.

Since childhood he had been frightened out of his mind. His father was rich and in 1919 had died of typhus in a concentration camp, and his aunt had emigrated to Paris with her husband, who was a general, and his elder brother had fought for the Whites. From his very childhood he had lived in terror. His mother had been frightened to the point of trembling before all authority—the militia, the apartment-house management, the apartment monitor, and the clerk at the city soviet. Each day and each hour he and his kinfolk had been made to feel their class inferiority and their class depravity. When he was in school, he had trembled before the cell secretary, kindly-appearing Galya, the Young Pioneer group leader. She, it seemed to him, looked upon him with revulsion, as if he were an untouchable worm. It horrified him that she might notice his adoring gaze.

And at this point one fact becomes comprehensible. A spell was cast on him by the might of the new world. Like a small bird hypnotized by a snake, he stared with lovely little eyes into the gleaming pupils of the all-powerful new world. He so much wanted to become a part of it, to be allowed to join it. And the poor little sparrow did not even peep or flap his wings when it turned out that his mind and his charm were needed by the dread new world. He offered his all on the altar of the Fatherland.

Now all this is true, of course! But what a fink he was! What a rat! In the course of acting as a stool pigeon he certainly did not forget to look out for himself. He had fine food. He basked in the sun. Nonetheless, he was very, very defenseless. A person like him ought not be let out without a nursemaid or a nice little wife. And just how was he to cope with a power that had caused half the world to bow down, that had turned a whole empire inside out? And he, with his tremulous delicacy, was like lacework. If you even touched him, he got all confused and frightened, and in his eyes would appear a fearful, hurt expression.

And yet this deadly swamp viper brought great torment to many people.

He did in people like himself, long-time friends, his dear, secretive, bright, shy friends. He alone had the key to them. He, after all, understood everything—he would weep when he read Chekhov's "The Bishop."

Yet let us go on pondering. Let us think this over fully. Let us not execute him before we have thought it over fully.

And here is a new comrade—Judas Number Three. He has an abrupt voice, somewhat hoarse, like a boatswain's. His gaze is searching, calm. He has self-assurance and is master of life. Sometimes they threw him into ideological work and sometimes into the fruit and vegetable trade. His questionnaire is as pure as the driven snow. He came from a family of lathe operators and the poorest of the poor peasantry.

In 1937 this man, without the slightest hesitation, wrote more than two hundred denunciations. His bloody list contained the most varied elements: commissars from the time of the Civil War, a poet-chansonnier, the director of a foundry, two district Party secretaries, an aged non-Party engineer, three editors, one of them on a newspaper and two from publishing houses, the manager of an official dining room, a teacher of philosophy, the head of a Party chancellery, a professor of botany, a lathe operator from an apartment-house management committee, two officials of the provincial agricultural department . . . It would take too long to list them all.

All his denunciations were directed against people loyal to the Soviet government, not against supporters of the czarist regime. His victims were members of the Party, men who took part in the Civil War, Party activists. His particular specialty was Party members of a fanatical frame of mind. He slit their eyes eagerly with a lethal razor blade.

Very few of the two hundred returned. Some were shot right away, and others were wrapped in a wooden overcoat —dead of dystrophy or shot in camp purges. Those who did return were crippled spiritually and physically. They are dragging out their lives somehow as best they can.

For him 1937 was a year of triumph. He was sharp-eyed, not-very-well-educated. It had seemed to him that everyone around him was stronger than he, both in education and in terms of a heroic past. Previously he hadn't a hope of ever scoring a point against those who had carried out the Revolution. But all of a sudden, with a kind of fantastic ease, he was able to mow down by his mere touch hundreds of those who wore haloes of revolutionary glory.

From 1937 on he himself climbed swiftly. He was the ultimate goal, the most priceless essence of the new era.

In his case, it would seem, everything is crystal-clear: he climbed to his high position as deputy or member of the Party Bureau by way of corpses and tortures.

But no, no, we must not hurry here either. We must sort it all out, we must ponder it carefully, before we deliver any kind of verdict. For he did not know what he was doing.

On a certain occasion his Party superiors said to him, in the name of the Party:

"We are facing catastrophe. We are surrounded by enemies! They pretend to be tried-and-true Party members, underground workers, participants in the Civil War, but they are actually enemies of the people, the heads of foreign intelligence services, provocateurs. . . ." The Party told him: "You are young and pure. I believe in you, fellow! Help me; otherwise I will perish. Help me win out over all this filth."

The Party screamed at him, stamped its Stalinist boots at him: "If you hesitate, then you are going to put yourself in the same category as those monstrosities, and I will grind you to a powder! Just never forget, you son-of-a-bitch, that 'black' chimneyless cabin in which you were born, and that here am I, leading you to the light! Hear and obey! The Great Stalin, your father, commands you: do them in!"

No, no, he was not settling personal accounts. And, though as a rural member of the Young Communist League, he did not believe in God, within him burned another faith—a faith in the mercilessly vengeful retribution of the great Stalin. Within him lived the unhesitating obedience of a believer. He appreciated and respected the mighty force and its great leaders, Marx, Engels, Lenin, and Stalin. As a soldier of the great Stalin he took his orders.

Yet, of course, within him, too, lived a biological dislike, an instinctive hidden loathing, for the people of the intellectual, fanatic, revolutionary generation whom he was told to do in.

He carried out his duty. He was not settling personal accounts. But he wrote denunciations out of a feeling of self-preservation as well. He was accumulating capital more valuable than gold and land—the trust of the Party. He knew that in Soviet life the trust of the Party means exactly everything: power, honor, authority. And he believed that his untruths served the supreme truth. His denunciations uncovered and revealed that truth.

How can he be accused when others wiser than he could not tell truth from falsehood, when even pure hearts could not in their impotence tell good from evil?

He, after all, believed, or, to be more precise about it, wished to believe, or, to be even more precise than that, was unable not to believe.

This whole dark deed was in some ways unpleasant to him, but after all it was his duty! Yes, and at the same time the awful deed also gave him pleasure, intoxicated him, held a strong attraction for him. "Just remember," his instructors told him, "you have no father, no mother, no brothers, and no sisters. . . . You have only the Party."

And the strange tormenting feeling intensified: in his blind obedience he acquired not impotence but dread might.

And in his evil eyes, which were like those of a general, in his abrupt, authoritative voice, seemed to flicker the glimmer of something quite different, of a secret personality—dazed, stunned, formed by the centuries of Russian slavery, by their Asiatic lack of freedom.

Yes, here, too, we have to think things over. For it is an awful thing to put to death even an awful human being.

But here is a new comrade—Judas the Fourth.

He lives in a communal apartment. He is an average, insignificant, white-collar employee; he is a collective farm activist. But no matter what his position, his face is always the same, be he old or young, ugly or a tall, dignified, ruddy giant of a Russian. He can be easily recognized anywhere. He is a philistine; he is greedy to acquire possessions; he is fanatically devoted to his material self-interest. His fanatic concentration on acquiring a sofa-bed, buckwheat grits, a Polish sideboard, construction materials in short supply, or imported textiles, is equal in its intensity to the fanaticism of Giordano Bruno and Andrei Zhelyabov.

He is the creator of a categorical imperative counterposed to that of Kant—for him human beings and humanity are invariably means to be employed in his search for objects. In his eyes, light or dark, there is a permanently tense, offended, irritated expression. Someone has always just stepped on his toes, and he is invariably engaged in settling accounts with someone.

The passion of the state for exposing enemies of the people was a find for him. It was like a trade wind on his ocean. His small yellow sail filled with the steady favorable breeze. And, through the sufferings of those he did in, he got what he needed: extra living space, an increase in salary, his neighbor's house, the Polish furniture, a heated garage for his Moskvitch automobile, a small orchard.

He despises books, music, the beauties of nature, love, and the tenderness of motherhood. He loves only things, just things.

He writes a denunciation against a fellow employee who danced with his wife and thereby made him jealous, against a wiseacre who made fun of him at dinner, and even against a neighbor who bumped into him accidentally in the apartment kitchen.

He has two particular and distinctive traits. He is a volunteer. No one scared him into it. No one compelled him to do it. And, in the second place, he sees quite clearly in his denunciations his own direct, plain, immediate material advantage.

Yet, for the moment, restrain that fist raised to strike him.

After all, his passion for objects is born out of poverty. He could tell you of a room eight meters square where eleven people sleep, where a paralyzed man snores, while next to him newlyweds rustle and moan, where an old woman mutters a prayer, and a child who has wet himself keeps crying.

He could tell you about greenish-brown village bread made from ground-up leaves, of being fed three times a day on a Moscow soup made of frozen potatoes that were slated to be thrown away as inedible.

He could tell you about a home where there was not one single pleasant object; chairs with plywood planking instead of seats; thick, low-grade, opaque glasses; tin spoons and forks with two prongs; underwear that had been patched and repatched over and over; a dirty rubber raincoat, worn in December over a tattered quilted jacket.

He could tell you about waiting for the buses in the morning darkness, of the implacable streetcar crush after the awful crowding at home.

Was it not his animal-like life that gave rise to his bestial passion for objects, for a more roomy den? Was it not because of his bestial life that he himself became a beast?

Yes, yes, that is all true, of course. But we must add that he lived no worse than others, that even though he lived badly, he still lived better than many, many others.

And many, many others did not commit what he committed.

Let us deliberate without haste here, and then we can arrive at our verdict.

Prosecutor: You confirm the fact that you wrote denunciations against Soviet citizens?

The Informers: Yes, in a way.

Prosecutor: Do you admit you are guilty of the deaths of innocent Soviet citizens?

Informers: No, we categorically deny it. The state had foredoomed those people to death, and our work, so to speak, was concerned only with the superficial framework. In essence, no matter what and how we wrote, whether we accused these people or declared them innocent, these people were foredoomed by the state.

Prosecutor: But sometimes you wrote denunciations on your own. In such cases you yourselves picked the victim.

Informers: That was just an apparent freedom of choice. People were destroyed in accordance with statistical methods, and the people scheduled for destruction belonged only to particular social and ideological strata. We knew these parameters. And, after all, you knew them too. We never informed against people who belonged to healthy strata that were not subject to destruction.

Prosecutor: To speak in terms of the Gospels: push those who are falling. However, there were cases, even in that harsh time, when the state acquitted people who had been slandered.

Defense Counsel: Yes, such cases actually did occur—as the result of a mistake. But, after all, only God makes no mistakes. Yes, and you can remember how rare the acquittals were; what that means is that mistakes were rare too.

Prosecutor: Yes, you informers knew your business. But nonetheless, answer me: why did you inform?

Informers *(speaking in turn):* They forced me. They beat me. . . . I was hypnotized by fright, by the power of boundless violence. . . . I was carrying out my Party duty as it was understood at the time.

PROSECUTOR: And what about you, Comrade Number Four, why are you silent?

JUDAS THE FOURTH: Why are you picking on me? I am not very bright or well educated. It is much easier for you to cast aspersions on me than on people who are educated and smart politically.

DEFENSE COUNSEL *(interrupting):* Permit me to make a clarification here. My client really did produce denunciations in pursuit of his personal aims. However, please take into consideration that his personal interests ran parallel to those of the state. The state did not reject the information provided by my client, and, consequently, it appears that he performed a useful function for the state, although at a first and superficial glance it might seem that he really produced denunciations out of selfish, personal considerations only. Here is the heart of the matter. In Stalin's time you yourself, Comrade Prosecutor, would have been charged with failure to value the role of the state highly enough. Do you realize that the powerful magnetic field created by our state, that its mass, with a weight of trillions of tons, and the superfear and supersubmissiveness which it induces in the human speck of dust are such as to make ridiculous any and every charge directed against a weak and defenseless individual human being? It is absurd to condemn a bit of fluff for having fallen to earth.

PROSECUTOR: Your view is plain: you do not choose to have your clients assume even the slightest trace of guilt. The state alone bears all the guilt. But tell me, informers, do not you yourselves, at least in some measure, admit to being guilty?

INFORMERS *(exchanging looks and whispering, whereupon the well-educated informer among them takes the floor on their behalf):* Let me reply. Your question, for all its seeming surface simplicity, is by no means so simple. First of all, it is meaningless, but that, as it happens, is of no significance. In actuality, why seek out now those guilty of crimes committed in the Stalinist era? That is like emigrating from the earth to the moon, and then bringing suit over a question of land boundaries on earth. On the other hand, if one considers that these epochs are not really so far distant from one another, and, as the poet said, in terms of historical ages, they stand virtually beside each other, then there arise many other complications. Why are you determined to expose particularly those like us who are weak? Begin with the state. Try *it!* After all, our sin is its sin. Pass judgment on *it*. Fearlessly, out in the open, out loud. You have no alternative, in view of how fearlessly you are speaking out on behalf of truth and justice. Well, get on with it! Act! And then explain one other thing, if you please. Why have you waited until now? You knew us all in Stalin's lifetime. You used to greet us cordially then and wait to be received at the doors of our offices, and sometimes while you waited you used to whisper about us in a birdlike voice. Well, we, too, whispered in birdlike voices. You, like us, were a participant in the Stalin era. Why should you, who were a participant, pass judgment on us, who were participants, and assess our guilt? Do you understand wherein the complexity lies? Perhaps we are guilty, but there is no judge who has a moral right to raise the question of our guilt. Recall the words of Lev Tolstoi: there are no guilty people in the world! But here, in our state, there is a new formula: the whole world is guilty, and no one is innocent. What is in question is solely the degree, the measure, of guilt. You have undertaken, Comrade Prosecutor, to bring charges against us. Only those who did not survive have the right to pass judgment on us. But dead men ask no questions and tell no tales. They are silent. So let us answer your question with another question. Man to man, human to human, straight and simple, in the Russian way. Wherein lies the cause of this universal, foul, unanimous weakness, submissiveness and compliancy, yours and ours?

PROSECUTOR: You are evading the question. *(The secretary enters and hands the well-educated police informer a document, saying: "From the government.")*

THE WELL-EDUCATED INFORMER *(after reading the paper):* I beg you: in connection with my sixtieth birthday my more than modest achievements in the field of Russian science have been honored.

PROSECUTOR *(reading the document):* Even against my will, I cannot but be glad for you—for after all we are all Soviet people.

THE WELL-EDUCATED INFORMER: Yes, yes, naturally, thank you. *(He mutters to himself:)* Permit me through the columns of your newspaper to thank . . . the institutions, the organizations, and also the comrades and friends . . . who have sent congratulations. . . .

THE DEFENSE COUNSEL *(strikes a pose and makes a speech):* Comrade Prosecutor, and you, honored jurors! The comrade prosecutor told my client that he had evaded replying when he asked wherein lies the cause of our general, universal, unanimous submissiveness and compliancy? Perhaps it was human nature itself that produced stool pigeons, police informers, slanderers. Perhaps they derive from the secretions of internal glands, or the squelching of liquids in the intestine or the rumble of digestive gases, or the mucous membranes, or the activity of the kidneys, or perhaps they arise from the blind instincts of food-seeking, self-preservation, propagation.

Well now, isn't it really immaterial whether stool pigeons are guilty or not? So they are to blame, so they are not to blame. So what! The thing that is loathsome, repulsive, is the fact that they exist. The entire animal, vegetable, mineral, physiochemical side of the human being is loathsome, repulsive. Because of that slimy, hairy, lower element of the human essence, stoolies come into being. Stool pigeons are born of human beings. The hot breath of fear of the state breathed upon mankind, and the slumbering seeds swelled and burst open. The state is the soil, the earth. And if the seeds were not hidden within the earth, neither wheat nor weeds would rise from it. The human being has only himself to thank for human dregs.

But do you realize the most loathsome thing about stool pigeons and informers? Do you think it is the evil that is in them?

No, not at all; the most awful thing is the good that is in them, the saddest thing of all is that they are replete with virtue, that they do good deeds.

They are loving, tender sons, fathers, husbands. They are quite capable of great achievements in doing good and getting work accomplished.

They love science, and our great Russian literature, and beautiful music, and some of them are equipped to express opinions on the most complex phenomena of contemporary philology and art.

And what devoted, loyal, good friends are to be found among them, and how considerately they visit a comrade who has had to go into the hospital!

What brave and patient soldiers are to be found among them! They shared their last crusts with their comrades, their last pinch of makhorka, and they took in their arms and carried off the battlefield fellow soldiers who were wounded and bleeding.

And what talented poets are to be found among them, and musicians, and physicists, and what talented lathe operators, too, and carpenters, the kind of whom people exclaim with delight: "Golden hands!"

Now that is what is really awful: the fact that there is so much good in them, in their human essence.

Who, then, is to be judged? Human nature! It gives birth to these piles of falsehood, vileness, cowardice, weakness. But it gives birth, too, to the good, the pure, the kind. The informers and the stool pigeons are replete with virtue; let them return to their homes; but how detestable they are with all their virtues, even with the complete remission of sins. Who was it who made that well-known bad joke: "Man, proud is thy name"?

Yes, yes, they are not guilty, they were forced to it by grim, gloomy, leaden forces, and trillions of tons of pressure were put upon them, and among the living there is no one who is innocent. All are guilty, including you, Comrade Prosecutor, and you, defendant, and I, who am considering the defendant, the prosecutor, and the judge.

But how shamed and how pained we must remain, face to face with our human indecency, unworthiness, obscenity!

8

"How could I have been so foolish as to go around town on foot?" Pinegin kept repeating to himself. He hadn't the slightest desire to think about that sinister sensation which had slumbered inside him for decades on end and had now suddenly awakened. For him the heart of the matter was not the evil deed, but the idiotic bad luck of meeting a human being he had ruined. Had they not run into each other on the street, the feeling asleep inside him would never have awakened.

But now it had, and Pinegin, without even sensing it himself, kept thinking less and less about his idiotic bad luck and became more and more alarmed and contrite: "Well, it's a fact I denounced Vanyechka, even though I could have sidestepped doing it, and I did break the man's back, damn him! In other circumstances we could have met and everything would have been all right. But now, good God, what a terrible taste I have in my mouth. As if I got caught in public with my hand in some woman's purse, as if she herself had grabbed my hand while my researchers and assistants, my secretary, my chauffeur were all standing around. How awful! After something that terrible, it would be impossible to go on living. My whole life is one big mess. I should have lived it quite differently."

This was Pinegin's confused state of mind as he entered an Intourist restaurant where he was well known to the maître d'hôtel, the waiters, and the doormen.

On seeing him, two checkroom attendants ran out whispering to him: "Welcome, welcome." And, neighing like colts, they reached out impatiently for the rich Pinegin accouterments. Their eyes were vigilant, the good eyes of bright native Russian lads working in an Intourist restaurant, very adept at recalling precisely who had been there, how he had been dressed, and what he had happened to say. But, to Pinegin, with his Soviet deputy's button, they had an openhearted attitude, almost as if he were their immediate superior.

Pinegin, feeling beneath his feet the soft, thick, resilient nap of the carpet, went on unhurriedly into the restaurant. A formal gloom hovered in the high, expansive hall. Pinegin breathed in slowly the air that was both cool and warm at once, glanced at the tables covered with starched tablecloths. The crystal vases held flowers; the beakers and glasses shone dully. He went on toward a familiar cozy corner beneath a fretwork of carved rhododendron. He passed between tables on which were displayed the flags of different countries of the world, and it seemed as if they were battleships and cruisers, and that he was the admiral on the flagship reviewing the fleet.

This feeling of being an admiral helped him go on living, and he sat down at the small table, and unhurriedly reached for the olive-green and dark blue menu which was as expensively produced as the official certificate for the winner of a big government prize, and when he had opened it, he peered attentively at the section headed "Cold Hors D'oeuvres."

On examining the names of the dishes listed in both Russian and the other major world languages, he turned over the crackling cardboard page and studied the section on "Potages," chewed his lips and then squinted at the section on "Meat and Wildfowl Entrees."

And at the very moment when he was stuck between the meat and wildfowl entrees, the waiter, guessing his problem, said: "The sirloin is excellent today."

Pinegin said nothing for a long time.

"If it's to be a sirloin, so be it," he said finally.

He sat in the semidarkness and silence with eyes half-closed, and the ponderous correctitude of his life argued with his embarrassment and horror—that suddenly awakened horror with the fire and ice of repentance.

Then the heavy velvet drapes on the door leading into the kitchen rustled, and Pinegin recognized his waiter by his bald head.

The tray floated out of the semidarkness toward Pinegin, and he could see on it the ash-rose of the smoked salmon surrounded with lemon slices, the darkness of the caviar, the hothouse green of the cucumbers, the steep sides of the vodka carafe, and the bottle of "Borzhomi" mineral water.

He was really not such a great gourmet as all that, nor was he all that hungry, but precisely at that moment the old man in his padded camp jacket ceased to trouble his conscience.

9

By the time he got to the railway station Ivan Grigoryevich felt that wandering about the streets of Leningrad had nothing more in it for him. He stood there in the chilly, high-ceilinged station and pondered. And some of those who walked past the gloomy old man staring at the black schedule board may have thought to themselves: "There he is, a man from camp standing at a crossroads, wondering which road to take." But, in fact, he was not selecting a destination at all.

Dozens of interrogators over the course of his life had understood quite clearly that he was no monarchist, no Social Revolutionary or Menshevik, that he had never been a part of either the Trotskyite or Bukharinist opposition. He had never belonged either to the new or to the old Orthodox Church, nor was he an adherent of the Seventh-Day Adventists.

At the station, thinking about his unpleasant days in Moscow and Leningrad, he remembered a conversation with a czarist artillery general who had lain next to him on the board bunks. The old man had said to him: "I do not intend to leave camp to go anywhere—it's warm here and people know me and I know them. And someone will always give me a piece of sugar and a *pirozhok* from a food parcel."

He had met such old men more than once. They no longer had any wish to leave camp. Camp was their home. Food was served at scheduled times. They received gifts from generous fellow inmates. There was a hot little stove to provide warmth.

And truly, truly, where were they to go on the outside? They kept deep within their hearts the brilliance of the chandeliers in the palaces at Tsarskoye Selo, the winter sun in Nice, and some even remembered Mendeleyev coming to have tea with their family, or had treasured memories of the young Alexander Blok, Scriabin, Repin. Like a warm glow within the ashes, some cherished recollections of Plekhanov, Gershun, Trigoni, of friends of the great Zhelyabov. There had been cases when old men released from camp had asked of their own accord to be readmitted—the storm of life had knocked them off their weak and trembling legs, and the impersonal chill of the enormous cities frightened them.

Ivan Grigoryevich wished he could return behind the barbed wire in order to seek out all those who had grown used to the camp work clothes, which, though tattered, were warm, to the camp gruel, to the barracks stove. He wanted to tell them that out in freedom it is really awful.

He would have told the weakened old men how he had visited his cousin, how he had stood outside the building in which the woman he loved lived, how he had run into a university friend who had offered his help. And he would have told the old camp people that there is no higher happiness than to be able to crawl on one's stomach, out of the camp, blind, one's legs amputated, and to die in freedom, even if only ten yards from the cursed barbed wire.

10

Ivan Grigoryevich fell into a mood of mingled relaxation and melancholy when he had finished calling at government offices in order to find a place to live and work, and when, employed in a southern city as a lathe operator in a metalworking artel for the handicapped, the sacred residence registration stamp appeared in his passport, and when he had actually taken up residence in the corner he had rented for forty-five old-style rubles a month in the home of the widow of Sergeant Mikhalyev, who had been killed at the front.

With Anna Sergeyevna, a thin, graying woman, yet not entirely gray and still young, lived her twelve-year-old nephew, son of her dead sister, pale of face, dressed in a patched, darned jacket, the astonishingly shy, quiet, and inquisitive sort of boy one finds only in a poor family. On the wall hung a photograph of Sergeant Mikhalyev—with a sad face, as if at the moment he was being photographed he had foreseen his unhappy fate. Anna Sergeyevna had a son of her own who was doing his compulsory military service in the convoy armies—units assigned to guard duty at camps, and elsewhere. His photograph showed him to be fat-cheeked, with his hair close cut by clippers, and it hung alongside his father's.

Sergeant Mikhalyev had been listed as missing in the first days of the war. The unit he had served in had been annihilated by German tanks not far from the border, and there was no one left to give evidence as to whether Mikhalyev had been shot down by German gunners and left dead and unburied on the battlefield or whether he had become a P.O.W. Therefore the authorities had refused his widow a pension.

Anna Sergeyevna worked as a cook in a mess hall. But she lived poorly, badly. Her elder sister, a member of a collective farm, had once sent her orphaned nephew a parcel from the village, consisting of shortbreads of black flour and bran, and a jar of honey with a lot of the wax still floating about in it.

Anny Sergeyevna, in her turn, sent food to her sister on the farm—flour, sunflower-seed oil, and white bread and sugar when she could get them.

It was hard for Ivan Grigoryevich to understand how Anna Sergeyevna could be so thin and pale in spite of working in a kitchen. In camp it was easy to recognize a cook among a crowd of prisoners—by his fat face.

Anna Sergeyevna did not ask Ivan Grigoryevich about his past life in camp. (He had been questioned in great detail by the personnel officer at the artel.) But Anna Sergeyevna, though she asked him nothing, kept observing Ivan Grigoryevich with eyes skilled in the understanding of life through having seen so much.

He had no difficulty sleeping on bare boards; he would

drink hot water without tea or sugar; he often munched dry bread; he wore footcloths inside his shoes in place of socks; he had no bed linen; but she noticed, at the same time, that the shirt he wore, though washed until it had turned pale yellow, had a clean collar, and that in the morning he got out a much battered and dented small box which had once contained fruit lozenges and cleaned his teeth with a brush, and carefully soaped his face, neck, and arms up to his elbows.

He found the silence at night strange. For decades past he had grown used to the multitudinous snores, puffings, mutterings, and groans of hundreds of people sleeping in barracks, to the knocking of the guards' clappers and the grinding of wheels. The only times he had been alone had been in punishment cells and once, in the course of an interrogation, when he had been kept in solitary for three and a half months.

Finding a job in the artel for the handicapped was a matter of pure luck. He had gotten into conversation in the city park with a tubercular man who was hunched over like a sled runner standing on end, and this man told him that he was about to give up his job as bookkeeper in an artel for the handicapped and was going to leave the city. He was leaving because he did not want to be buried in a city where the cemetery was located in a swamp and the coffins floated in their watery graves. The bookkeeper wanted to be buried in full comfort. He had saved up his money for an oak coffin. He had bought some red funeral cloth to line it and accumulated a stock of small brass nails of the sort used to upholster the leather divans in railroad stations. He had not the slightest desire to be immersed in water along with all these possessions.

And he spoke about all this in the voice of a person about to move to a new, more comfortable apartment.

In his own mind Ivan Grigoryevich christened this old fellow "the housewarmer." And it was on his recommendation that Ivan Grigoryevich was taken on as a lathe operator in the artel, which produced locks and keys, and tinned and soldered kitchenware. Ivan Grigoryevich's technical skill was useful there—at one time he had been a lathe operator in a camp repair shop.

Among the workers were war invalids, people crippled in accidents at work or on public trolley-buses, and even three old men mutilated back in World War I. There was even an old camp veteran there, Mordan, a former worker in the Putilov Factory. He had been sent up on Section 58 in 1936 and was released only after the end of World War II. Mordan did not want to return to Leningrad where his wife and daughter had died in the siege. He had settled in with his sister in this southern city and become a worker in the artel.

The handicapped in the artel were for the most part merry people inclined to take a humorous view of life. But sometimes one or another of them would have a fit or fainting spell. And amid the roar of the hammers and the screeching of the files one would hear the screams of the epileptic, who had begun to beat the floor.

The gray-mustached tinsmith Patashkovsky was a war prisoner of the 1914 war (it was said of him that he was an Austrian who pretended to be a Pole). Suddenly his arms would go numb and dead, and he would freeze there on his stool with his hammer raised in the air, his face immobile and supercilious. He had to be jerked by the shoulder to bring him out of his fit. And on one occasion a fit of one of the handicapped people set off a chain reaction among the others, and all over the shop old people and young began to beat the floor and scream.

Ivan Grigoryevich experienced a totally new feeling that he found astonishing, marvelous. He was working as a free, hired worker—without jailers or watchtowers, without convoy guards marching him out to work and back. And it was strange: the work was apparently the same, the tools were apparently the same familiar tools; and yet no one called anyone else a shit and there were none of the veteran Russian thieves threatening one, nor any "bitch" trusties hanging around shaking their cudgels.

Ivan Grigoryevich quickly saw the devices the employees used to increase their meager earnings. Some made pans and teapots out of materials they had bought on their own. These were sold through the artel, at the price set by the state, no higher and no lower. Others made private agreements with customers for outside repair jobs, and were paid directly. There were neither bills nor receipts exchanged; they were paid for their work exactly what the state paid—no more, no less.

During a lunch break, Mordan, a man with hands as large as snow shovels, told them about a big fuss in his apartment house. Five neighbors all lived in the same communal apartment next door to his—a lathe operator, a tailor, a machine-shop repairman, and two widows; one of the latter worked at a garment factory and the other was a charwoman in the city soviet. On their day off both widows were hauled into the militia station; both had been picked up by detectives from the "Department for the Fight Against Theft of State Property and Speculation" for selling on the street net bags which they would weave at home at night, each woman keeping it a secret from the other. The militia thereupon conducted a search of the apartment, and it turned out that at night the tailor was engaged in making boys' and women's coats; the repairman had an electric hotplate under the floor on which he baked wafers that his wife sold on the open market; the lathe operator from the Red Torch Factory turned out to be a nighttime shoemaker, manufacturing women's shoes; and the widows wove not only net bags but also women's sweaters.

Mordan made his listeners laugh as he described how the repairman screamed that he was baking the wafers for his family and the inspector had asked whether he needed for his family the seventy-two pounds of flour he had on hand. Each violator had been fined three hundred rubles, and reports had been filed on each at his or her place of work, and all of them had been threatened with being exiled from the city so as to purge Soviet life of—believe it or not—"parasites and nonworking elements."

Mordan loved using learned words in his conversation. When he examined a damaged lock, he would say in a very weighty way: "Yes, indeed, the key does not react at all to the lock." Or, as he walked down the street after work alongside Ivan Grigoryevich, he would suddenly say: "It was not only because of the death of my wife and daughter that I decided not to return to Leningrad. I simply cannot stand seeing with my own eyes the fate of the Putilov proletariat. They can't even strike. And what kind of workers can they be if they haven't got the right to strike?"

In the evening Anna Sergeyevna, his landlady, would bring home some food for her nephew in her bag—a jar of soup and a main course in a dish.

"Maybe you would like something to eat?" she asked quietly of Ivan Grigoryevich. "We have enough."

"I can see for myself that you eat nothing at all," he replied.

"I spend the whole day eating; that's the kind of work I do," she replied, and then, apparently understanding his look, she said: "I get very, very tired at work."

During his first days there his landlady's pale face seemed to Ivan Grigoryevich unkind. Later he sensed that she was, in fact, kind. On occasion she would tell stories about life on the collective farm. She had been a brigadier and once she had even been farm chairman for a while. The collective farms had failed to fulfill the plan—either because they had not planted enough, or because there was a drought, or because they had overtaxed the land and it had lost its strength, or because all the men and young people had gone off to the city. And since the plan for deliveries to the government had not been fulfilled, the farmers had received only six or seven kopecks for a workday, plus perhaps three and a third ounces of grain. And there were years when the farmers didn't even get a single ounce. But the fact is that people don't want to work for nothing. The collective farmers just plain stopped working. They ate clean black bread, without such additives as ground potatoes and acorns, on holidays only, as if it were cake. Once Anna Sergeyevna had brought some white bread to her sister on the farm, and the children found it so strange they had been afraid to eat it. It was the first time in their lives they had seen such a wonder. Their log huts were falling apart. There was no construction timber available to them.

He listened to her and looked at her. From her shone the precious light of kindness and femininity. For decades he had seen no women, and for long years he had listened to the endless barracks stories about women—bloody, sad, dirty. And the women in those stories were either so degraded as to be lower than animals, or so pure and elevated as to be a cut above the women saints. But to think about women was just as unalterably necessary to the prisoners as their bread ration, and was omnipresent in their conversation, and in both their pure and impure dreams.

Ivan's reaction to Anna Sergeyevna seemed strange to him, for after his liberation he had seen beautiful, well-dressed women on the streets of Moscow and Leningrad; he had sat at table with Mariya Pavlovna, a beautiful gray-haired woman. And yet neither the grief which overwhelmed him when he learned that the love of his youth had betrayed him, nor the beauty of the well-dressed city women, nor the atmosphere of self-satisfaction and comfort in Mariya Pavlovna's home had aroused in him the intensity of feeling he experienced as he listened to Anna Sergeyevna, and looked into her sad eyes, or at her near and dear face, pale but at the same time young.

And yet there was nothing strange about this either. What was taking place between Ivan Grigoryevich and Anna Sergeyevna had been taking place between other men and women from the beginning of time.

She had explained to Ivan Grigoryevich:

"I could not bear to drive hungry people out to work. Lenin had me in mind when he said that a housewife should be able to run the state. The farm women used to work at the thresher, and they used to make themselves a special kind of stocking which they sewed into the hem of their skirt, and they would pour grain into it. It was my job to have them searched and to have charges brought against them! And the minimum sentence for the theft of such collective farm property was seven years! Those women had small children. I used to lie there and think about it—the state was taking the grain from the collective farm for six kopecks a kilo and selling baked bread for one ruble, and in our collective farm not even one ounce of the grain they had grown or of the bread made from it was issued to the farmers for four whole years. Just what do you call that? A peasant grabbed a fistful of grain that he himself, no matter how you figure it, had sowed. And for that he got seven years. No, I just couldn't go along with it! Well! So my friends and fellow countryfolk got me a job in the city as a cook. Here I feed people. And the workers say: 'Despite everything it's better in the city.' Construction workers have a norm of two and a half rubles for hanging a door or putting in a lock—for doing the same work on a private basis on their day off, they get fifty. The state pays a construction worker one-twenty-fifth of what he gets from a private customer for the same work. And the state takes even more than that from the peasants. What I think is that the state takes too much from both. I understand all about rest homes, and schools, and tractors, and defense—I understand it all, but they take too much, they should take less."

She looked at Ivan Grigoryevich.

"Perhaps all our life is on the wrong footing because of that."

Her eyes slowly passed from his face to her nephew's face and she said: "Of course, I know that one is not supposed to speak of such things. But I can see what kind of person you are. So I asked you. And you don't have the slightest idea of what kind of person I am, so you don't need to answer."

"Why not? I will," said Ivan Grigoryevich. "I used to think freedom was freedom of speech, freedom of the press, freedom of conscience. But freedom is the whole life of everyone. Here is what it amounts to: you have to have the right to sow what you wish to, to make shoes or coats, to bake into bread the flour ground from the grain you have sown, and to sell it or not sell it as you wish; for the lathe operator, the steelworker, and the artist it's a matter of being able to live as you wish and work as you wish and not as they order you to. And in our country there is no freedom—not for those who write books nor for those who sow grain nor for those who make shoes."

At night Ivan Grigoryevich lay there and listened in the darkness to someone's sleepy breathing. It was so light that Ivan Grigoryevich was not certain whose it was, the child's or the woman's.

And, strangely, it now seemed to him as if he had been in motion from place to place all his life, as if night and day he had been listening endlessly to the click of train wheels, and that here at long last he had finally arrived—his prisoner transport had come to a halt at its final destination.

But as a result of thirty years of this life of continuous motion, thirty years of the roar and thunder of the road, a noise and a ringing in his ears kept on sounding inside his head, and it seemed to him as if the train were rolling on and on and on. . . .

11

Alyesha, Anna Sergeyevna's nephew, was so short that he could easily have been taken for an eight-year-old. He was in the sixth grade in school, and when he came home, he used to fetch the water and wash the dishes and then sit down to study his lessons.

Sometimes he would look up at Ivan Grigoryevich and say: "Quiz me, please, on my history lesson."

When Alyesha was studying biology, Ivan Grigoryevich, because he had nothing else to do, began to model small figures of the various animals shown in the textbook: a giraffe, a rhinoceros, a gorilla. Alyesha was dumfounded. Those beasts of clay seemed marvelous to him. He used to look at them over and over and move them from place to place, and at night he would put them on the chair next to his bed. One morning, at dawn, as he was leaving to get in line for milk, the boy asked in an anxious whisper: "Ivan Grigoryevich, can I take your animals to school?"

"But, of course; they are yours," said Ivan Grigoryevich, who was washing up in the hallway.

That evening Alyesha told Ivan Grigoryevich that his drawing teacher had said: "Tell your boarder he must study art."

Anna Sergeyevna, who for the first time saw Ivan Grigoryevich laugh, said: "Why don't you go see that teacher? Don't laugh! Maybe you can earn money at night. What kind of life is it anyway—on three hundred and seventy-five rubles a month!"

"It's all right. I don't need any more!" said Ivan Grigoryevich. "Anyway, the time for me to have done my studying was thirty years ago."

And he thought to himself: "Why worry? You're alive, aren't you, you're not dead, right?"

Once Ivan Grigoryevich told Alyesha about Tamerlane's great campaign, and he noticed that Anna Sergeyevna had put aside her mending and was listening attentively.

"You shouldn't be working in an artel," she laughed.

"Where else?" he said. "The knowledge I possess comes from a book with many pages torn out of it, without a beginning or an end."

Alyesha deduced that this must be the reason why Ivan Grigoryevich thought up things in his own special way, whereas his teachers repeated their stories from a textbook that did have a beginning and an end.

But the droll little episode of the clay figurines excited Ivan Grigoryevich. He did not, of course, possess any real talent, or so he felt. But there were so many people whose deaths he had witnessed, so many who had been wrapped up and buried in a "wooden overcoat," so many young physicists, historians, connoisseurs of ancient languages, philosophers, musicians and composers, young Russian Swifts and Erasmuses who had perished.

Prerevolutionary literary critics had so often mourned the fate of the serf actors, musicians, composers, and painters, who had been unable to develop their talents because they were slaves. But who in the books of the present time has yet sighed over or mourned those young men and women who, because they died or rotted in camps, never had the opportunity to paint their pictures or write their books? The Russian land gives birth with great fecundity to its Platos and its quick-witted Newtons, but how horribly and easily it devours its own children.

What he saw in the theaters and the movies filled him with boredom and revulsion. It seemed as if someone were using main force to make him look at the stage or the screen—and that he could not escape it. Many of the novels and verses he read aroused in him the intolerable sensation of forced feeding. It was as though their authors were writing about some totally different and unfamiliar life—a life with no punishment barracks, no camp brigadiers, no jailer-turnkeys, no security officers, no system of internal passports, a life from which the real feeling, suffering, passion, and fear by which all those around him lived were utterly absent.

Writers dreamed up out of whole cloth people and their feelings and thoughts. They dreamed up out of whole cloth the rooms in which they lived, the trains in which they traveled. The literature which called itself "realistic" was just as formalized and imaginary as the bucolic romances of the eighteenth century. The collective farmers, workers, and rural women of Soviet literature seemed, in fact, to be close kin to those beautifully built villages and those curly-headed shepherdesses who played on pipes and danced in the meadows among pure-white lambs bedecked in sky-blue ribbons.

Ivan Grigoryevich, during the years he had spent in camps, had learned much about human weaknesses. Now he saw that there were plenty of them on both sides of the barbed wire. Suffering did not always purify. The struggle for an extra swallow of camp soup, for an easy assignment or exemption from work, was cruel, and weak-willed people descended to a pitiful level. And now in freedom Ivan Grigoryevich could easily guess how one or another haughty and carefully groomed man must have scavenged about, scraping his spoon in the dirty mess kits of others, or hunted around the kitchen in his search for slops, potato peelings, and rotten cabbage leaves.

His pity had been stirred by those people, broken and crushed by violence and cruelty, by hunger, by cold, by being deprived of tobacco, who had been transformed into camp "jackals," who kept a sharp lookout to grab off a bread crust or a slimy cigarette butt.

And people in freedom helped Ivan Grigoryevich to understand camp people. In freedom he could see their miserable weakness, their cruelty, their greed, their fear, all the very same emotions he had seen in camp. The human beings were the same, and he pitied them.

In novels and poems Ivan Grigoryevich could see that Soviet people were being depicted like people in medieval art, who had represented the Church's ideal, the idea of divinity: they proclaimed the one and only true God; and the human individual existed only in order to glorify God and His Church. And certain writers who were adept in presenting falsehood as truth went to great lengths to trace with particular care and precision the details of actual clothing and furnishings, and then went on to people their accurate, realistic stage sets with their own imagined, God-seeking heroes whom they had dreamed up out of whole cloth.

Both in freedom and in camp people did not want to admit that they were equal in their right to freedom. Certain right-deviationists considered themselves innocent, but regarded the repressions applied to the left-deviationists as altogether just. The right- and left-deviationists both hated the "spies"—those who corresponded with their relatives abroad, those whose Russified parents and ancestors bore Polish, Latvian, and German family names.

And no matter how firmly the peasants in camp insisted that they had worked all their lives with their own hands, the political prisoners refused to believe them: "We know they would never have agreed to liquidate poor peasants."

Ivan Grigoryevich said to a former commander of Red Guard troops who had the neighboring bunk: "You dedicated and devoted your whole life to the ideals of Bolshevism, and you are a hero of the Civil War. And here you are serving time and charged with espionage."

And the answer was: "In my case they made a mistake. Mine is a special case. It simply cannot be compared with others."

When the Russian thieves picked out a new victim to be plundered and, perhaps, knocked off, and began to torment him and to steal from him, some of the political prisoners simply turned their heads away, while others just sat there, and still others pulled their blankets over their heads and pretended to be sleeping.

Hundreds of prisoners together, among them former soldiers and war heroes, were helpless against a few of the veteran criminals. The thieves committed outrages, considering themselves patriots and the political prisoners "fascists"—enemies of the Motherland. People in camp were like dry grains of sand. Each for himself, to himself.

Some, for example, believed there had been a mistake only in their own case, that as a rule "they did not arrest a person for no reason at all."

Others had things figured out this way: "When we were free, we used to assume that they did not arrest anyone without a reason, and now we know that they do!" But they drew no broader conclusions from this and sighed submissively.

An emaciated, twitchy former official of the Youth Comintern, a hair-splitter and dialectician, explained to Ivan Grigoryevich that he had committed no crimes against the Party, but that the security organs were right in arresting him as a spy and a double-dealer. For even though he had committed no crimes he nonetheless belonged to a stratum hostile to the Party, a stratum which had given rise to double-dealers, Trotskyites, opportunists, whiners, complainers, and skeptics.

On one occasion in camp an intelligent inmate who used to be a Party official on the province level got into a conversation with Ivan Grigoryevich:

"When they chop down the forest, the chips fly, but the Party truth remains the truth and it is superior to my misfortune. And," he went on, pointing to himself, "I myself was one of those chips that flew when the forest was cut down."

And he was nonplused when Ivan Grigoryevich said to him: "That's where the whole misfortune lies—in the fact that they're cutting down the forest. Why cut it down?"

Only very rarely did Ivan Grigoryevich encounter in

the camps people who had actually struggled against the Soviet government.

Former czarist officers had ended up in camp, but not because they had formed an underground monarchist organization. They were in prison because they might have tried to do so.

There were Social Democrats and Social Revolutionaries in the camps. Many had been arrested when they were merely trying to eke out a living, when they were politically inactive, and when in fact they were not disloyal to the government. They had been arrested not because they were struggling against the Soviet state but because they might struggle against it.

The peasants were sent to the camps not because they had opposed the collective farms. Those who were sent might, under certain conditions, oppose the collective farms.

People got sent to camp for innocent criticism. One might not have liked the books and plays awarded prizes by the state, and another might not have liked Soviet-made radios and fountain pens. Under certain conditions such people, too, might have become enemies of the state.

People were sent to camp for corresponding with aunts and brothers who lived abroad. They were sent there because the possibility of their becoming spies was greater than in the case of those who had no relatives beyond the borders.

Terror was directed not against those who had committed crimes but against those who, in the opinion of the punitive apparatus, had a slightly greater likelihood of committing them.

Distinct from such prisoners were people genuinely hostile to the Soviet government who had really fought against it: elderly Social Revolutionaries, Mensheviks, Anarchists, or advocates of the independence of the Ukraine, Estonia, Lithuania, and, during the war and postwar period, the Ukrainian Nationalist Banderists.

Soviet prisoners considered them their enemies, but they were nonetheless fascinated by people who had been imprisoned for actual due cause.

In a hard-labor camp for political prisoners, Ivan Grigoryevich had met an adolescent student named Borya Romashkin, who had been sentenced to ten years in prison because he had actually written leaflets accusing the state of persecuting innocent people, and he had really typed them out on a typewriter, and he himself had actually posted them at night on the walls of apartment buildings in Moscow. Borya had told Ivan Grigoryevich that during the course of his interrogation dozens of officials of the Ministry of State Security, among them several generals, had come to take a look at him. All were interested in this boy who had been arrested for due cause. In the camps Borya was even famous. Everyone knew about him. Prisoners from nearby camps all asked about him. When Ivan Grigoryevich was sent off on a prisoner transport to a new camp eight hundred kilometers away, he had heard the story of Borya Romashkin on his very first evening there—news of him had traveled to the ends of the country, even as far as the Kolyma itself. But the surprising fact was that the people who had been imprisoned and sentenced for due cause, for active and genuine opposition to the Soviet state, thought that all the political zeks were innocent, that all of them, without exception, should be freed. But those who had been framed and imprisoned on the basis of cooked-up, fake charges—and there were millions of them—were disposed to propose an amnesty only for themselves, and made every effort to confirm the authentic guilt of all the other falsely accused "spies," "kulaks," and "wreckers"; they were quite willing to excuse the cruelty of the state.

There was one profound difference in emotional makeup between people who were in prison and those in freedom. Ivan Grigoryevich could see for himself that in camp people remained faithful to their own particular period. Various epochs of Russian life lived on in the character and thoughts of each. Here were men who had taken part in the Civil War, with their favorite songs, heroes, books; here were to be found "greens"—peasant partisans—and Petlyura supporters, with the undimmed passions of their own time and their own songs, verses, and customs; here were officials of the Comintern of the twenties, with their own pathos and vocabulary, with their own philosophy and way of bearing themselves and pronouncing their words; here were very old people—monarchists, Mensheviks, SR's—and all of them preserved within themselves an entire world of ideas, manners, and literary heroes that had existed forty and fifty years before.

It was quite easy to recognize in a tattered, coughing old man, a downhearted, seedy, yet generous and decent officer of the Czar's household cavalry, and, similarly, to identify in the equally tattered man in the next bunk, his face overgrown with gray bristle, an unrepentant Social Democrat; one might sense in a stooped hospital orderly a commissar of a Civil War armored train.

In contrast, elderly people in freedom did not display the obvious signs of their past; in them the past had been erased, wiped out, and they merged easily into the landscape of the new era. They thought, suffered, and experienced the world in a contemporary way; their vocabulary, thoughts, passions, and even their form of sincerity had changed compliantly, elastically, in tune with the course of events and the will of the state.

What explained this difference? Perhaps in camp, as if under anesthesia, a person came to a total standstill in time?

Living in camp, Ivan Grigoryevich constantly saw people's natural striving to get out from behind the barbed wire, to be released, and returned to their wives and children. But in freedom he sometimes met people who had been released from camp, and their submissive hypocrisy, their fear of their own thoughts, their dread of being arrested again were so overwhelming that they seemed to him more truly prisoners than they had been in camp.

On getting out of camp, and living as freely hired workers beside human beings near and dear to them, they sometimes doomed themselves to a kind of imprisonment more absolute than that of camp: one more perfected and profound.

For despite everything, even with all the torments and tortures, in the dirt, muddiness, and murk of camp life, the light and the strength of heart of the men in camp lay in freedom. Freedom was deathless.

In this small city, living in the home of Sergeant Mikhalyev's widow, Ivan Grigoryevich began to feel the meaning of freedom more intensely and inclusively.

In people's day-to-day struggle to live, in the extreme efforts workers put forth to earn an extra ruble through moonlighting, in the collective farmers' battle for bread and potatoes as the one and only fruit of their labor, he could sense more than the desire to live better, to fill one's children's stomachs and to clothe them. In the battle for the right to make shoes, to knit sweaters, in the struggle to plant what one wished, was manifested the natural, indestructible striving toward freedom inherent in human nature. He had seen this very same struggle in the people in camp. Freedom, it seemed, was immortal on both sides of the barbed wire.

Once, after work, he began to go over in his mind special camp words. My Lord, there was one for each letter in the alphabet. And one could write essays, poems, novels about each of them.

"A" for arrest; "B" for barracks; "C" for camp—and so on and so forth, down to the very end of the alphabet. Camp was an enormous world. It had its own language, its own economics, its own moral code. One could fill whole bookshelves with works about it. More shelves even than one could fill with the *Histories of Factories and Mills* which Gorky had initiated.

Here, for example, is a subject: forming up a train of prisoner-transport cars for a journey across Siberia and guarding that train.

How innocent and comfortable to today's transported prisoner the prisoner transports of the twenties seem, the political prisoner in a compartment of a passenger car, accompanied by a guard who was also a philosopher and who used to provide the prisoner with *pirozhki.* Those were the shy, tender beginnings of the camp culture, the gray stone age, a chick which had hardly emerged from the egg.

And the present-day sixty-car train traveling to Krasnoyarsk Territory: a mobile prison city, four-axle railway freight cars, tiny barred windows, triple-decker bunks; warehouse cars, staff cars full of jailers; kitchen cars; cars with police dogs that encircle the train when it stops; the chief of the transport, surrounded, like a fairy-tale pasha, with fawning cooks, with concubine-prostitutes.

Then there are the prisoner counts and searches: one jailer climbs into a car containing prisoners while the other jailers stand with automatic pistols aimed at the crowded clump huddled inside and herded into one end of the car; and the count proceeds by driving one designated prisoner at a time from the crowded end of the car to the empty end; and no matter how quickly the prisoner dashes across, the jailer always manages to strike a blow either on his rump or his crown.

And not long ago, after the Great War of the Fatherland, steel prongs were placed underneath the rear cars. And if a prisoner managed to saw through the flooring during the journey and throw himself flat between the rails, the steel comb would grab him, tear him apart, and drop him under the wheels; for those who broke through the ceiling of the car and climbed out on the roof, there were searchlights whose dagger-like beams pierced the darkness from the locomotive to the end car; there was a machine gun pointed the length of the train just in case a man should run along the roof, and that machine gun knew what it was there for. Yes, everything changes and develops. The economics of the train had crystallized too: the officers of the convoy troops established so comfortably in the headquarters car, the food for them and their men stolen in part from the rations for prisoners and dogs; the especially big travel allowances paid the convoy troops, in consideration of the sixty days it took the train to reach the Eastern Siberian camps; the internal-trade turnover, involving the thieves' stealing from the political prisoners and selling their plunder to the jailers and guards; the consequent harsh capital accumulation and the parallel pauperization within this one single train.

Yes, everything was forever flowing, forever changing, and every prisoner train was and will be different from the one before and the one coming after. One can never enter the same train twice.

And who will describe the desperation of that forward motion separating men from their wives, those nighttime confessions to the tune of the iron click of the wheels and the rattle of the cars, the submissiveness, the trust, the sinking into the camp abyss, letters thrown from the cars in the dark into the murk of that great mailbox which is the Russian plain (letters that arrived at their addresses too, believe it or not)?

Aboard the train, camp customs and habits have not yet been established; the camp frame of mind, so continually muddled with trouble and worry, has not yet developed. For the bloodied heart everything is unfamiliar, and everything is awful—the half-light, the creaking, the rough boards, the grabbing thieves, the quartzlike stare of the convoy guards.

Someone lifted a small lad up to the tiny window and he shouted out: "Grandfather, Grandfather, where are they taking us?"

And everyone in the car listened to the old man's long-drawn-out voice: "To Siberia, dear, to hard labor."

All of a sudden Ivan Grigoryevich thought: "So this was my path, my fate! With these trains my road began. And it has now come to its end here."

Those recollections of camp which often arose without any apparent connection tormented him with their chaotic character. He believed and he felt that one can after all make sense out of chaos too, that it was within his power to do just that; and that now that his road through camp had come to an end, the time had come to perceive clearly, to discern the laws within the chaos of suffering, the contradictions between guilt and holy innocence, between falsely confessing to one's crimes and fanatical loyalty, between the meaninglessness of murdering millions of innocent people who were devoted to the Party and the iron meaning of those murders.

12

Lately Ivan Grigoryevich had said little. He talked hardly at all with Anna Sergeyevna. But at work he often thought of her and kept looking at the wall clock which hung in the lathe shop to see how soon he could leave.

And, for some reason, in these silent days, as he thought of life in camp, he kept remembering the fate of women in camps. Never, it seemed, had he thought so much about women.

Russian women's equality with men had not only been established in postgraduate courses in the universities, and in the works of sociologists. Women's equality with men had not only been established by working in factories, by flights into outer space, and in the fire of revolution. It had been established in the history of Russia, now, heretofore, and for all time to come, by suffering in serfdom, camp, prisoner transports, and imprisonment.

In the enserfed ages, and in the Kolyma, Norilsk, and Vorkuta, women had become equal with men.

Camp also confirmed a second truth that was as simple

as a commandment of the Gospel: the life of men and women is indivisible.

There is a satanic force in a prohibition, in a barrier, a dam. The water of streams and rivers backed up by a dam manifests a dark and secret force of its own. This hidden force can be concealed for a time by lovely sand, by patches of sunlight, by the rocking of water lilies, and can then appear in an instant, and the implacable anger of the water crushes stone and drives the blades of the turbine with insane speed.

Pitiless is the power of starvation if a dam divides a human being from his bread, his food. The natural and beneficent need for food is tranformed into a force that destroys millions of lives, a cruel and bestial ferocity that compels mothers to eat their children.

A prohibition separating women from men in camp warps their bodies and souls.

Everything in a woman—her tenderness, her concern, her passion, her motherliness—constitutes the bread and the water of life. All this arises within a woman because there are men in the world: husbands, sons, fathers, brothers. All this makes the life of a man complete because there are women—wives, mothers, daughters, sisters.

But suddenly a commandment, prohibiting men in the life of women and women in the life of men, is put into operation. And everything simple and good—the bread and the water of life—suddenly reveals hidden springs of darkness and malevolence.

As though by sorcery, a prohibition imposed by force inevitably transforms good into evil within the human being.

Between the women's camp and the men's camp for ordinary criminals lay a ribbon of vacant land called an open-fire zone. Machine guns opened fire as soon as anyone appeared in this no-man's land. Nonetheless the criminals used to crawl across the open-fire zone on their bellies; they dug tunnels beneath it; they wriggled under the barbed wire; they climbed on the barbed wire itself; and those who did not make it across lay with broken legs and bullet holes in their heads. It recalled the insane, tragic urge of salmon to swim up their spawning rivers even when they are blocked by dams.

There were special hard-labor camps for women in which for long years no man's voice had been heard. And if it happened that some male lathe operator, truck driver, or carpenter was sent into these camps on special assignment, he might be torn apart, unimaginably tormented, killed by the women. The men criminals feared as one fears fire those camps where it was considered happiness merely to touch the body of a dead man with one's hand. They were afraid to go there even with a special armed guard.

Dark, somber, grim misfortune twisted people at hard labor, transformed them into nonhumans.

In the hard-labor camps for women some women forced other women into perverted cohabitation. In the hard-labor camps for women absurd types emerged—women stud dogs, bull dykes—with deep, husky voices, a long male stride, and male gestures, dressed in britches and in soldiers' jackboots. And alongside them were those lost and pitiful beings—their "females."

The "stud dogs" drank superstrong concoctions of tea, like the men criminals, using it to get stoned; they smoked makhorka, and when they were drunk they beat up their cheating, light-minded girl friends; but they also guarded them with their fists and their knives, protecting them from the insult and injury of others, and from crude passes by other women. These tragic and ugly relationships were what love turned into in hard-labor camps. It was monstrous. It provoked neither laughter nor dirty talk, but sheer horror even in the hearts of the thieves and the murderers.

In hard-labor camps the frenzy of love refused to recognize distances across the taiga, or barbed wire, or masonry walls, or punishment blocks, or gatehouse watches, or prison locks.

It would defy the wolf-killer police dogs, razor blades, and the shots fired by the camp guards. In exactly the same way, salmon, with eyes popping out of their sockets and humped-up backbones, push up to their spawning grounds, flinging themselves upward against the crags and boulders of mountain rapids and waterfalls.

At the same time the camp people hung onto their love for their wives and mothers; and camp "correspondence brides," who never had seen and never would see the camp "grooms" they had chosen, were prepared to accept any torture for the sake of that pretense of marriage they had devised.

Something can be forgiven a person who, in the dirt and stink of camp violence, remains a human being.

13

Quiet Mashenka! She was no longer wearing her thin stockings and her navy-blue woolen sweater. It was hard to keep neat in a prisoner-transport freight car. She kept listening, straining her ears, trying to understand the strange talk of the women thieves, her bunk neighbors; it almost seemed a different language. She looked in horror at the queen of the train—the hysterical, pale-lipped mistress of a famous gang-chief of Rostov thieves.

Masha tried to wash her kerchief in her cup, and with the last bit of water in it she bathed her feet. She spread the kerchief to dry on her knees and peered out into the half-darkness. Everything was mingled, in the fog before her eyes, all the last months and other things too: Yulya's tears after she had eaten too much on her third birthday a few years before; the faces of the state security men while searching their room—linens, drawings, dolls, dishes strewn about the floor; the ficus plant pulled out of its pot, lying on the floor—the ficus her mama had given them as a wedding present; her husband's last smile from the threshold of the room, pitiful, imploring her to be true and loyal. Remembering that smile, she clasped her head in her hands and sobbed. Then followed the insane weeks when everything was the same, except that all the time, along with little Yulya's hot cereal, there was the icy horror of the Lubyanka; queues in the reception office of the Internal Prison at the Lubyanka and a voice from the window: "No parcels permitted." Scurrying around to relatives, memorizing the addresses of kinfolk and friends; the hurried and awkward sale of a wardrobe with a mirror, and of the fine editions put out by the Academia publishing house; pain when her best friend stopped phoning her; and those nighttime guests once again, and the search lasting till dawn; saying farewell to little Yulya, whom they had, in all likelihood, not turned over to her grandmother but had probably taken to an orphans' home. Then the Butyrka Prison, where everyone spoke in a whisper, where matchsticks or fishbones, picked out of the gruel, were made to serve as needles for one's mending, the varicolored sight of dozens of washed kerchiefs, panties, bras, being waved in the air as the imprisoned women tried to dry them. There was an interrogation, and for the first time in her life men had shaken their fists at her, addressed her insultingly by the intimate personal pronoun, and cursed her as a "whore, a prostitute." She was charged with having failed to denounce her husband, and he had been sentenced to ten years without the right of correspondence for failing to denounce to the police some alleged terrorist activity.

Masha simply could not understand why she and dozens like her were supposed to denounce their husbands, why Andrei and hundreds of others like him were supposed to denounce their comrades at work, their childhood friends.

The interrogator summoned her only once. And then eight months passed in prison—day and night and night and day. Desperation shifted to a dull waiting for her fate; and then suddenly, like an ocean wave, her hope, her assurance that she would soon be reunited with her husband and daughter, subsided.

Finally the jailer handed her a narrow slip of cigarette paper on which she read: "Section 58–6–12."

But even after this she still kept hoping. All of a sudden they would repeal the sentence. Her husband would turn out to have been acquitted. Yulya would be there at home. And they would meet again, never again to be separated. And she turned hot and cold with joy at the mere thought of this encounter.

At night they awakened her: "Lyubimova, with your things!" They took her in the Black Maria, bypassing the usual stay in the Krasnopresnya Transit Prison, directly to the Yaroslavl Line freight station to be loaded onto her prisoner-transport train.

She could recall with particular clarity the morning following her husband's arrest, just as if that morning were still continuing.

The main entrance door to the apartment house had slammed shut, a motor roared, and silence fell; horror gripped her heart. The telephone rang in the corridor; the elevator suddenly came to a halt on the landing outside their apartment door; and one of their neighbors, her slippers slapping the floor, went from the kitchen; and suddenly the slapping sound of the slippers halted.

She wiped the books scattered about the floor with a dustcloth and put them back on the shelf; she tied the linen lying on the floor into a bundle—she wanted to boil it because everything in the room seemed to have been dirtied. She put the ficus back in its pot and stroked its leathery leaf. Andryusha had laughed at this ficus and considered it a symbol of philistinism, and in her soul she agreed with him. But Masha never permitted him to insult the ficus and never allowed him to move it to the kitchen. She was sorry for her poor mother—her mother, quite old, had carried it all the way across Moscow to present the gift to them, and she had even hauled it up to the fifth floor all alone, because the elevator was not working.

Everything was silent! But the neighbors were not sleeping. They pitied her, and they were afraid of her, and they were overjoyed that they were not the ones for whom the police had come with a warrant for search and arrest.

Little Yulya was asleep at last and Mashenka was picking up the room. Ordinarily she did not try so hard to keep things picked up. By and large she was indifferent to things. She never cared about chandeliers or lovely china. Some people considered her to be a bad housewife, slovenly. But Andrei liked Masha's indifference to things and the disorder that reigned in their room. Yet right now it seemed to her somehow that if only things were put in their proper places, she would then be more relaxed and it would be easier for her.

She glanced into the mirror and looked about the room she had finished tidying. *Gulliver's Travels* was right there in the bookshelf where it had been yesterday, before the search. The ficus was once again in its pot on the table where it had been before. And little Yulya who had wept and clung to her mother until four, was slumbering. There was silence in the corridor. Their neighbors were not as yet making any noise in the kitchen.

And in her newly neat room Mashenka felt a sharp pang. She was all aglow with tenderness and love for Andrei, and then and there, in that domestic silence, surrounded by all her familiar objects, she felt, as never before, the merciless force which was capable of bending the axis of the earth. This force had pierced her directly, pierced little Yulya, and entered the tiny room of which she had once said: "I don't need twenty square meters and a balcony, because I am happy right here."

Yulya! Andryusha! She was being taken away from them! The click of the wheels bored into her soul. She was being taken farther and farther away from Yulya, and with every hour Siberia was coming closer, and it was Siberia that they were now giving her in place of life with those she loved.

Mashenka was no longer wearing her checked skirt. The woman thief over there with the pale thin lips was combing out her electric hair with Mashenka's comb.

Doubtless it is only in the heart of a young woman that two particular torments can exist at one and the same time: that of the mother possessed by the passionate desire to save her helpless child, and that of the self become a helpless child when face to face with the state, yearning to hide her head on her own mother's breast.

Those dirty and broken fingernails were once so very carefully manicured, and little Yulya at six had been so fascinated by their color, and on one occasion Andrei had said to his daughter: "Your mother's fingernails are like fish scales." And no trace of her permanent remained either. She had had her hair done a month before Andryusha's arrest because she was getting ready to go to a birthday party at her girl friend's house—the very same friend who had stopped ringing her up on the telephone.

Yulenka, Yulenka, shy, nervous—in an orphan's home. Masha moaned quietly and plaintively and objects grew dim before her eyes. How could she protect her daughter against cruel orphanage attendants, against naughty, malicious children, against rough and tattered orphanage clothing, against the rough soldier's blanket and the prickly straw-stuffed pillow? And the railway car kept creaking, and the wheels kept clicking on the rails, and Moscow was getting farther and farther away, Moscow and Yulya, and Siberia ever closer.

Good Lord, had all of this really happened? Maybe it was all a dream; this fetid, stifling semidarkness, this aluminum bowl, these women thieves smoking their makhorka on the harsh bunk boards, this dirty underwear, this itching body, and this heartache. "If we could just stop somewhere soon, then at least the guards would defend us against the women thieves." And then when there actually was a stop, there was only terror at the sight of flourished guns and the cursing guard, and immediately one thought: "If only we would get moving again." And the thieves themselves would say: "The Vologda convoy guard is worse than death itself."

But it was not in the creaking bare board bunks, nor in the frost that appeared on the car walls as soon as the stove went out, nor the cruelty of the guards, nor the outrages committed by the women thieves, that her real misfortune lay.

It lay in the fact that there in the railway car the numbness of heart which had lasted throughout her eight-month incarceration in prison had begun to ebb.

And as a result she felt with all her being the nine thousand kilometers of her journey into the Siberian graveyard depths.

She no longer held that meaningless yet ever-present prison hope that the cell door would open and the jailer would cry out: "Lyubimova, take your things. You are being released." Or that she would come out of the Butyrka onto Novoslobodskaya Street, and board a bus and return to her home where Andrei and Yulya would be waiting for her.

In the railway car that prison-cell numbness was altogether absent; so, too, was the simple, mindless fatigue of camp; there was only her bloodied, aching heart.

And she kept thinking: What if little Yulya should wet her panties, and what if she needed to have her hands washed, and what if her nose needed to be blown, and then, too, what about the fact that she always needed vegetables, and that she always threw off the bedclothes at night and slept uncovered and exposed to the cold?

Mashenka no longer wore her own nice shoes. Instead, she had on soldier's boots—and the sole was torn off one of them. Could it really have been she, Mariya Konstantinovna, Mashenka, who used to read Blok, who had been a philology student, and who, without ever telling Andrei, had written verses of her own? Had it really been she, Masha, who would run to the Arbat to make an appointment with the hairdresser, Ivan Afanasyevich, also known as "Jean"? The very same Mashenka who not only read books, but also knew how to make excellent borsch, and bake French pastry, and sew, and who had fed her child so well? Masha, who had always delighted in Andryusha, in his diligence, in his modesty, and had in turn delighted everyone around her with her faithful love for Andrei and Yulya? Masha, who knew how to weep and how to have fun and how to make people laugh and how to laugh herself and how to economize in small ways?

And the train kept going on and on and Masha began to come down with typhus. Her head was dim and dizzy, heavy. But, no, she did not have typhus, it turned out; she was all right. And once again, there in the prisoner-transport train, hope found a path to her heart. They would all arrive at the camp and an officer would shout: "Lyubimova, step forward from the ranks. There is a telegram here for you—you have been released." And so on and so forth and all the rest that went with it. And she would be sent to Moscow in a passenger train and she would see again the Moscow suburbs of Sofrino, Pushkino, and then the Yaroslavl Station, and there she would see Andrei and hold Yulya in her arms.

And hope aroused heartache. If only they would arrive at their Siberian destination sooner so that she could get that telegram about her release! How Yulya's thin little legs hurried and ran. She was running alongside the train as the railway car began to slow down.

And here is Masha, disembarking from the train at last—plundered by the women thieves, hiding her freezing fingers in the sleeves of her greasy padded jacket, her head bound about with a dirty Turkish towel. And beside her, the shoes of hundreds of Moscow women, who like her have been sentenced to ten years in camp for failing to denounce their husbands, creak glassily on the crust of the snow.

Feet still in silk stockings march forward and stumble on

high heels. They envy Masha too—because she has traveled in a car with thieves, not just with other "wives." She has been robbed of her own clothes, but, as a result, she now possesses a padded jacket, and she can stuff paper and rags into her soldier's boots to keep her feet warm.

The wives of the enemies of the people stumble and hurry. In haste they try to gather up their possessions, lying scattered on the snow, and tie them back into their knotted bundles, but they are afraid to weep.

Masha looks about her. Behind her are a station shed, railway freight cars strung out like red beads on a snow-white body, and up ahead a dark snake turns and twists—a column of women prisoners; all around them are piles of lumber covered with snow, and convoy guards dressed in marvelously warm sheepskin coats, while the police dogs, warm in their own thick fur, keep barking and barking.

And the air, which, after two months of being closed up in a freight car, is ravishingly clean, is meaner than a razor blade in its sharp blast. The wind rises and a dry snowy mist is driven across the virgin land, and the head of the column has already drowned in the white mist. Masha's head whirls.

And all of a sudden, through the fatigue, through the fear of frostbite and gangrene, through the dream of getting someplace warm and washing up in a bath, through the confusion up ahead because some massive old woman wearing pince-nez was lying there in the snow with a strange, idiotically whimsical expression on her face, the twenty-six-year-old Masha could see her camp fate in the snowy mist. And at the same time, she could also see that behind her, thousands of versts back, in Spasopeskovsky Lane a police seal now dangled on her former fate. Out of the mist loomed the watchtowers, with their guards in full-length sheepskin overcoats, and the open gates. In that moment Masha saw both her lives with the same bright clarity: the life which had gone and the other which had arrived.

She ran and stumbled and blew on her icy fingers, and even now the insane hope did not leave her—they would get to the camp, and when they did, the people there would tell her that the papers ordering her release had come. That, in fact, was why she ran so hard that she was panting from the exertion.

What hard work they gave her! How her stomach muscles and the small of her back ached from the enormous weight of the big chunks of limestone, illegal for women to lift according to the labor laws; and the handbarrows, even when empty, seemed as heavy as though they were made of iron. How heavy were the spades, the crowbars, the boards, the beams, the tanks full of dirty water, the latrine barrels full of sewage, and the great heaping piles of wet laundry.

How hard was the march to work in the predawn mists, in the darkness. How hard it was to endure being searched by the guards in slush, mire, and intense cold. How nauseating, and yet how longed for, the corn mush with a shred of entrails in it, the putrid fish scales clinging to one's palate; how viciously, pitilessly, they stole in the barracks; what filthy conversations took place at night on the bunks; what loathsome goings-on, whispers, and rustling took place there; how eternally desirable was the stale black bread touched with gray.

The woman thief Mukha, who worked in the boiler room and who lay next to Masha on the board bunks, began to cohabit with sixteen-year-old Lena Rudolph. Lena became infected with syphilis, and she lost her fingernails, and her head went bald, and the medical department transferred her to a camp for invalids, while Lena's mother, the kind, bright-eyed, obliging Suzanna Karlovna, who even in camp had preserved her daintiness, kept right on working even though she was gray-haired. She used to do her exercises before dawn every day and would rub herself down with snow.

Masha used to work until dark, like a mare, a she-donkey, a she-camel. The camp was a hard-labor camp. Masha did not have the right to receive or write letters. She did not know whether her husband had been executed or was still alive, nor where little Yulya was, whether she had been turned over to an orphanage, whether she had been lost like a nameless little beast, or whether her grandmother had found her. Nor, for that matter, did she know whether her own mother was alive or whether her brother Volodya was alive. It was as if she had grown used to knowing nothing of her relatives and friends. She did not even dream of getting a letter. She wanted lighter work, which would not take her out into the cold, into the taiga where bloodsucking insects devoured one. She wanted work attached to the kitchen, to the hospital.

Her longing for her husband and her daughter went right on and on and her hope did not die. It only seemed to; it merely slumbered for a while. And Masha felt her dream, just as one feels a sleeping child in one's arms, and when hope awakened, the young woman's heart was filled with happiness, with light, with grief.

She would see Yulya and her husband once again. Of course, not today and not tomorrow. Years would pass, but she would see them; how gray you have become, what sad eyes you have. Yulenka, Yulenka! This pale, thin little girl was her daughter! And Masha would worry whether Yulya would recognize her, whether she would remember her, her camp mama, whether she might not turn away from her.

The senior jailer Semisotov forced her to have sex with him. He knocked out two of her teeth and struck her a blow on the temple. That happened her first autumn in camp. She tried to hang herself, but she couldn't carry it out. The rope turned out to be rotten, and broke. There were certain women who even envied her Semisotov. And she finally achieved a state of pained indifference. Twice a week she dragged herself behind Semisotov into the stockroom to some wooden bunks covered with sheepskin. Semisotov was always gloomy, grim, silent, and she was frightened of him to the point of going out of her mind. She would even get sick to her stomach and vomit from fear when he was drunk and became enraged. But one time he gave her five pieces of candy, and she thought to herself: "If only I could send them to Yulya in the orphanage." So she did not eat them and hid them in her straw mattress. And of course they were stolen. One time Semisotov said to her: "You're filthy, you whore! A peasant woman would never let herself get so dirty." He always addressed her with the formal personal pronoun, even when he was dead-drunk. Semisotov's disgust gladdened her, and yet she thought: "If he throws me out, I am going to be sent out to work at that limestone again."

Semisotov went away one night and never returned. She found out later he had been transferred out of the camp. And she was glad when she could sit on her bunk in the barracks at evening without having to follow him, with hanging head, to the stockroom. But then she was fired from the office where, under Semisotov, she used to wash floors and keep the stove fueled. After all, there was no reason to coddle her any longer. And her job was taken over by that same woman thief who had stolen her woolen sweater on the prisoner-transport train. Masha was glad, but felt hurt at the same time; he hadn't even said a word in farewell. He had treated her worse than a dog. But, after all, she had once possessed permanent registration in Moscow and had lived in a separate, individual room with her husband and with Yulya! She used to be able to bathe in their own apartment bathroom, and she used to eat from a plate.

The camp work during the winter months was very hard. Work in the summer was also hard. And on spring and autumn days it was hard to work. And she no longer thought about the Arbat district where she had lived, nor about Andrei, but only about the fact that while she had been with Semisotov she had washed floors in the office. Was this really her fate?

Yet deep inside her, hope remained. She would see her family once again. Of course, by then she would look like an old woman and be completely gray. Yulya would have children of her own—but they would see each other someday. They would, of course.

Her head was filled with worries, fears, troubles; her shirt got torn. Then she got boils. Then her stomach ached, and she was unable to get permission to go to the medical department. And suddenly the skin on her heels burst and she was lame. And her footcloths grew black from blood spots. And her felt boots began to fall apart. And then she simply had to get washed up, at least a little bit, without waiting her regular turn.

She had to have at least a tiny chance to wash her clothes, or at least to dry out her quilted cotton jacket, which had gotten wet in the rain. And she had to fight for every little thing—a pot of hot water, thread to darn with, a needle rented out to her, a spoon with a complete handle, some strips to use for patches. How could she save herself from the gnats, how could she protect her face and her hands from the frost, which was as mean and vicious as the camp convoy guard?

But the cursing, the quarrels, the fights of the imprisoned women were no easier to bear than the camp work.

And the barracks life kept on and on.

Aunt Tanya, a charwoman from Orel, used to whisper: "Grief to those who live on the earth." She had the crude face of a peasant. Her faith seemed ecstatic, cruel. But there was no cruelty or frenzy in her, just kindness. Why had this saint been sent to camp? With unbelievable kindness she was quite ready to take anyone else's place at washing floors or at serving a duty period.

The old nuns Varvara and Kseniya, in contrast, used to whisper only to each other and then fall silent as soon as any sinful nonbeliever came near. They lived in their own special world. It was a sin for them to sign any piece of paper, or to utter their real nonreligious names, to drink from the same cup as lay people, to put on a camp jacket. They would let themselves be killed before consenting to any of these things—so stubborn were they in their holiness. Their holiness was visible in their clothing, their white kerchiefs, their tightly pursed-up mouths; their eyes held coldness and contempt for camp suffering, for sinfulness. To their holy, elderly virginity, the women's passions all around them, the women's misfortunes, the sufferings of mothers and wives, were repulsive, and it all seemed to them unclean. For them the main thing was to preserve the cleanliness of their kerchiefs, of their cup, and to avoid with their pursed-up lips the sinful camp life. The women thieves hated them, and the "wives" had no special affection for them either.

Wives, wives—Moscow wives, Leningrad wives, Kiev wives, Kharkov wives, Rostov wives—sad, some of them down-to-earth and practical and some of them not of this world at all, sinful, weak, meek, vicious, some of them much given to laughter, Russian and non-Russian, women in camp jackets. Wives of physicians, engineers, artists, and agronomists, wives of marshals and of chemists, wives of prosecutors and of independent farmers exiled during the liquidation of the kulaks, Russian, Byelorussian farmers. All of them had followed their husbands into the Scythian murk of the camp burial mounds.

And the more famous the "enemy of the people" who had perished, the wider was the circle of women who departed in his wake on the path to camp: the wife, the former wife, the very first wife of all, sisters, secretaries, daughters, women friends of his wife, daughters from his first marriage.

Of some it was said: "She is surprisingly modest and unassuming." And of others: "She is an insufferable, haughty, high and mighty lady, as if she were in a special Kremlin category even here." Such women had their hangers-on here too, their "poor relations and dependents." Over them hovered the aura of power and doom. Of them it was said in a whisper: "No, you can be sure those women will never get out alive."

There were old women with tired and relaxed eyes who

had been imprisoned way back in Lenin's time and who had added up whole decades of prison and camp life. These were the narodnaya volya women, the Social Revolutionaries, the Social Democrats. They were held in respect by the guards. Even the women thieves were respectful to them. They would not rise from their board bunks even if the camp chief himself entered the barracks. It was said of one of them, Olga Nikolayevna, a tiny, gray-haired old woman, that before the Revolution she had been an Anarchist and had thrown a bomb at the carriage of the governor of Warsaw, that she had shot at a gendarme general. And here she was now, sitting on the camp bunk boards and reading a booklet and drinking hot water from a mug. On one occasion, Masha returned at night from the stockroom where Semisotov had taken her, and this old woman came up to her and stroked her on the head and said: "My poor little girl." And Masha had sobbed and sobbed.

And not far from Masha, Suzanna Karlovna Rudolph lay on a bunk. Her husband, a professor, an Americanized German, was a Christian Socialist who had come with his family to Soviet Russia and taken out Soviet citizenship. Professor Rudolph had been sentenced to ten years without the right of correspondence and had been shot in the Lubyanka. Suzanna Karlovna and her three daughters, Agnes, Louise, and Lena, had all been sent to hard-labor camps. After the youngest of them, Lena, had been packed off to the invalids' camp with syphilis, Suzanna Karlovna refused to exchange greetings with Olga Nikolayevna, because Olga Nikolayevna had called Stalin a fascist and Lenin "the assassin of Russian freedom." Suzanna Karlovna claimed that her work was helping to build the new world and this gave her the strength to bear being parted, for the time being, from her husband and daughters. Suzanna Karlovna described how, when she lived in London, they had been friends of H. G. Wells, and how in Washington they had met President Roosevelt, who had enjoyed talking with her husband. She accepted everything, and everything was quite clear to her except one thing: when they had come to arrest him, she had seen Professor Rudolph put a big gold coin in his pocket, the only one they had, the size of a child's hand, a one-hundred-dollar piece with the profile of an Indian in war feathers on one side. And she had noticed how the man conducting the search had taken away the coin for his young son, without even stopping to consider that it might be gold.

All of them—the pure and the fallen, the tormented and the strong—lived in hope. Hope sometimes slumbered and sometimes it awakened. But hope never left them.

And Masha hoped. Hope pained her. But because she had hope she was still able to breathe even in her pain.

After the harsh Siberian winter, which seemed as long as a camp term in itself, the pale spring came. And one day Masha was sent out, with two other women, to fix the road which led to the new "socialist settlement" where the chiefs and the free employees of the camp lived in log cottages. From far off she could see her own curtains on the tall windows there in the settlement, just as on the Arbat, and the silhouette of her ficus. She could see a small girl carrying her schoolbag climb up on the porch and go on into the house belonging to the man in charge of administration of the hard-labor camps.

The convoy guard said to her: "What do you think you're here for—to look at movies?" And when, in the light of the setting sun, she was going back to the camp, near the lumber warehouse, the Magadan radio station began to blare out.

Masha and the two other women who were dragging their way along, squelching through the mud, put down their spades and stopped.

Silhouetted against the sky stood watchtowers, and the sentinels in their black sheepskin coats perched on them like great enormous flies, and the low flat barracks looked as though they had once started to grow out of the ground and then reconsidered: perhaps they ought to grow back into the ground.

The music was not sad but gay: dance music. And Masha wept when she heard it as she had never wept in her life. The two women standing next to her wept too. One was a peasant woman sent up during the campaign against the kulaks, and the other was an elderly Leningrad woman in spectacles with cracked lenses. And as she wept it seemed as if even the cracks in her spectacles had come from those tears.

The convoy guard didn't know what to do. After all, prisoners wept very rarely. Their hearts were frozen, like the tundra, in hard permafrost.

He pushed them in the back and chided them: "All right, all right! That's enough! Shit! Your mother! Come along as you're supposed to, you whores! Please!"

He kept looking around, and the idea never entered his mind that the radio music was the reason the women were sobbing.

Nor did Masha herself understand why her heart was suddenly filled with anguish and desperation. It was as if everything that had ever happened in her life had come together all at once. Her mother's love. The checked woolen dress she liked so very much. Andryusha. The beautiful verses. The ugly snout of that interrogator. Dawn over the suddenly gleaming blue sea at Kalasuri near Sukhumi. Yulya's chatter. Semisotov. The old nuns in camp. The crazy quarrels of the "stud dogs." The ache in her heart because their woman brigadier had begun to look at her, narrowing her eyes persistently, the same way Semisotov had. Masha just didn't understand why suddenly, when she heard the gay dance music, she had begun to feel the dirty undershirt on her body, her shoes as heavy as irons, the sour stink of her pea jacket, why, suddenly, the question slashed her heart like a razor blade: To what end, for what, why, for her, all this endless cold, all this spiritual degradation, all this submissiveness that had developed within her toward her fate at hard labor?

Hope, that had always pressed its living, vital weight upon her heart, had died.

To the tune of the gay dance music, Masha lost once and for all the hope of ever again seeing Yulya, adrift somewhere in the network of orphanages and children's colonies in the immensity of the Union of Socialist Soviet Republics. To the tune of the gay music, young people were dancing in their dormitories and clubs. But Masha understood at last that her own husband did not exist any more, that he had been shot, that she would never see him.

And she was left without hope, all alone. Never would she see her Yulya, not today, nor as a gray old woman, never!

Lord, Lord, have mercy upon her, Lord, have mercy upon her . . .

In a year's time Masha left the camp. Before returning to freedom she lay in a freezing dugout on a pine board bench, and no one tried to force her to go out to work, and no one insulted her there. The morgue assistants placed Masha Lyubimova in a rectangular box made out of boards rejected by the lumber inspectors for any other use. For the last time they looked upon her face. On it was an expression of gentle, kind, childish triumph and dismay, that very same expression her face wore at the lumber warehouse when she heard the gay dance music—when she had first felt joy and then had understood there was no hope for her.

And Ivan Grigoryevich thought to himself that at hard labor in the Kolyma men were not equal to women. Despite everything, the fate of the men was easier.

14

Ivan Grigoryevich saw his mother in a dream. She was walking along a road, keeping to one side to be out of the way of a long moving line of tractor trucks and dump trucks. She did not see her son. He cried out to her: "Mama, Mama, Mama." But the heavy roar of the tractors drowned out his voice.

He had no doubt at all that in the noise and bustle of the highway she would still recognize her son in the gray-haired camp veteran, if only she could hear him, if only she would turn around.

In desperation he opened his eyes. Bending over him was a woman in a nightdress. He had called his mother in his dream, and the woman had come to him.

And now she lay alongside him. He felt instantly, with all his being, how beautiful she was. She had heard him cry out in his sleep, and she had come to him, overflowing with tenderness and pity. There were no tears in her eyes, but he saw in them something more than sympathy. He saw in them what he had never before seen in the eyes of a human being.

She was beautiful because she was kind, good. He took her by the hand. She lay there beside him. And he felt her warmth, her tender bosom, her shoulders, her hair. It seemed to him that he perceived all this not waking but in a dream, asleep. Awake, in his waking hours, he had never ever been happy.

She was all goodness, kindness, and he comprehended with his fleshly essence that her tenderness, her warmth, her whisper were beautiful because her heart was full of kindness for him, because love is goodness and kindness.

This was their first night as lovers. It was on this night that she told him her story:

I don't want to remember it. It is terrible. But I can't forget it. It just keeps on living within me; whether or not it slumbers, it is still there. A piece of iron in my heart, like a shell fragment. Something one cannot escape. I was fully adult when it all happened.

Darling mine! I loved my husband very much. I was pretty. But I was not a nice person, not kind. I was twenty-two. You would not have fallen in love with me then even though I was pretty. I know. As a woman, I can feel it. I am more to you than simply someone who has been in bed with you. I look upon you—don't be angry with me for saying this—as Christ. I keep wanting to repent to you as God. My wonderful one, my love, I want to tell you all about it, to pour out the whole thing, everything that happened.

No, there was no famine during the campaign to liquidate the kulaks. Only the horses died. The famine came in 1932, the second year after the campaign to liquidate the kulaks.

I used to wash the floors in the Workers and Peasants Inspection Headquarters, and my friend used to wash them in the agricultural department. We learned a lot. I can tell you exactly how it all happened. The accountant told me: "You should be a minister." I really do grasp things quickly, and I have a good memory.

The campaign to liquidate the kulaks began at the end of 1929, and the height of the drive came in February and March of 1930.

I can remember well: before they were arrested, a special assessment was levied on them. They paid it once, finding the money somehow or other. And then it was levied on them a second time—and those who had anything left to sell sold it, anything to be able to pay up. They thought that if only they paid up, the state would forgive them. Some of them, however, slaughtered their cattle and distilled illicit vodka from their grain—and ate and drank everything up. They said it didn't make any difference. There was no life left for them anyway.

Perhaps in other provinces things went differently. But in our province here is exactly how it happened. They began to arrest the heads of families only. Most of those arrested first had served in the cavalry under Denikin. The arrests were carried out solely by the GPU. Party activists had no part in this at all. All those rounded up in this first stage were shot—to a man.

Those arrested at the end of December were held in prison for two or three months and then sent off to special resettlement colonies. And at this period, when the fathers of families were arrested, the other family members were left untouched, but an inventory of their property was drawn up, and the family living in the household was no longer considered to own what belonged to it but merely to have been put in charge of it for safekeeping.

The province authorities sent the plan down to the district authorities—in the form of a total number of "kulaks." And the districts then assigned proportionate shares of the total number to the individual village soviets, and it was in the village soviets that the lists of specific names were drawn up. And it was on the basis of these lists that people were rounded up. And who made up the lists? A troika—three people. Dim-witted, unenlightened people determined on their own who was to live and who was to die. Well, that makes it all clear. *Anything* could happen on this level. There were bribes. Accounts were settled because of jealousy over some woman or because of ancient feuds and quarrels. And what kept on happening was that the poorest peasants kept getting listed as kulaks while those who were more prosperous managed to buy themselves off.

Now, however, I can see that the heart of the catastrophe did not lie in the fact that the lists happened to be drawn up by cheats and thieves. There were in any case more honest, sincere people among the Party activists than there were thieves. But the evil done by the honest people was no less than that done by the dishonest ones. These lists were evil in themselves; they were unjust. It was all the same who got included in them. Ivan was innocent, and so was Peter. Who had established the plan's master figure for the whole of Russia? Who had ordered this plan for the entire peasantry? Who had signed it?

The fathers were already imprisoned, and then, at the beginning of 1930, they began to round up the families too. This was more than the GPU could accomplish by itself. All Party activists were mobilized for the job. They were all people who knew one another well and knew their victims, but in carrying out this task they became dazed, stupefied.

They would threaten people with guns, as if they were under a spell, calling small children "kulak bastards," screaming "Bloodsuckers!" And those "bloodsuckers" were so terrified they had hardly any blood of their own left in their veins. They were as white as clean paper. The eyes of the Party activists were glassy, like the eyes of cats. They were in the majority after all, and they were dealing with people who were acquaintances and friends. True, they were under a spell—they had sold themselves on the idea that the so-called "kulaks" were pariahs, untouchables, vermin. They would not sit down at a "parasite's" table; the "kulak" child was loathsome; the young "kulak" girl was lower than a louse. They looked on the so-called "kulaks" as cattle, swine, loathsome, repulsive: they had no souls; they stank; they all had venereal diseases; they were enemies of the people and exploited the labor of others. And, on the other hand, the poor peasants, the members of the Young Communist League, and the militia—they were all Chapayevs, heroes of the Civil War. Yet these activists were in reality ordinary people like all the rest; many of them were just plain whiners and cowards; and there were plenty of ordinary scoundrels as well.

These slogans began to have their impact on me too. I was just a young girl. And they kept repeating them at meetings and in special instructions and on the radio; they kept showing them at the movies; writers kept writing them; Stalin himself, too: the kulaks are parasites; they are burning grain; they are killing children. And it was openly proclaimed "that the rage and wrath of the masses must be inflamed against them, they must be destroyed as a class, because they are accursed." And I, too, began to fall under the spell of all this, and it began to seem as if everything evil had sprung from the kulaks and that if they were destroyed a happy time would instantly ensue for the peasantry.

And there was no pity for them. They were not to be regarded as people; they were not human beings; one had a hard time making out what they were—vermin, evidently. I became a member of the Party activist committee too. The activist committee included all kinds—those who believed the propaganda and who hated the parasites and were on the side of the poorest peasantry, and others who used the situation for their own advantage. But most of them were merely anxious to carry out orders from above. They would have killed their own fathers and mothers simply in order to carry out instructions. And the worst were not those who really believed the destruction of the kulaks would bring about a happy life. For that matter, the wild beasts were not the most poisonous among them either. The most poisonous and vicious were those who managed to square their own accounts. They shouted about political awareness—and settled their grudges and stole. And they stole out of crass selfishness: some clothes, a pair of boots. It was so easy to do a man in: you wrote a denunciation; you did not even have to sign it. All you had to say was that he had paid people to work for him as hired hands, or that he had owned three cows. I was aroused and unhappy, but I did not suffer deeply. It was as if the cattle on a farm were being slaughtered in violation of the rules. I was unhappy, of course, very much so! But I did not lose sleep over it.

Do you remember how you answered me? I will not forget your words. One can tell they were daytime words. I asked you how the Germans could kill Jewish children in gas chambers, how they could go on living after that. Could it be that there would be no retribution, either from God or from other people? And you said: only one form of retribution is visited upon an executioner—the fact that he looks upon his victim as something other than a human being and thereby ceases to be a human being himself, and thereby executes himself as a human being. He is his own executioner. While the man who has been done in, has been executed, remains a human being for all eternity, no matter how he has been murdered. Do you remember that?

So now I understand why I came here to be a cook. Why I did not want to be a collective farm chairman. Yes, I have spoken of this before.

And nowadays I look back on the liquidation of the kulaks in a quite different light—I am no longer under a spell, and I can see the human beings there. But why had I been so benumbed? After all, I could see then how people were being tortured and how badly they were being treated! But what I said to myself at the time was "They are not human beings, they are kulaks." And so I remember, I remember and I think: Who thought up this word "kulak" anyway? Was it really Lenin? What torture was meted out to them! In order to massacre them, it was necessary to proclaim that kulaks are not human beings. Just as the Germans proclaimed that Jews are not human beings. Thus did Lenin and Stalin: kulaks are not human beings. But that is a lie. They are people! They are human beings! That's what I have finally come to understand. They are all human beings!

And so, at the beginning of 1930, they began to liquidate the kulak families. The height of the fever was in February and March. They expelled them from their home districts so that when it was time for sowing there would be no kulaks left, so that a new life could begin. That is what we all said it would be: "the first collective farm spring."

It is clear that the committees of Party activists were in charge of the expulsions. There were no instructions as to how the expulsions should be carried out. One collective farm chairman might assemble so many carts that there would not be enough household possessions to fill them up. They called them "kulaks," but they went off in half-empty carts.

From our village, on the other hand, the "kulaks" were driven out on foot. They took what they could carry on their backs: bedding, clothing. The mud was so deep it pulled the boots off their feet. It was terrible to watch them. They marched along in a column and looked back at their huts, and their bodies still held the warmth from their own stoves. What pain they must have suffered! After all, they had been born in those houses; they had given their daughters in marriage in those cabins. They had heated up their stoves, and the cabbage soup they had cooked was left there behind them. The milk had not been drunk, and smoke was still rising from their chimneys. The women were sobbing—but were afraid to scream. The Party activists didn't give a damn about them. We drove them off like geese. And behind came the cart, and on it were Pelageya the blind, and old Dmitri Ivanovich, who had not left his hut for ten whole years, and Marusya the Idiot, a paralytic, a kulak's daughter who had been kicked by a horse in childhood and had never been normal since.

In the district center there was no space left in the prisons. Yes, and when you get down to that, what kind of prison was there in the district center anyway? A hole in the wall. And there were many more coming than just this one column—a column from each village. The movie theater, the club, the schools were all inundated with prisoners. But they did not keep them there long. They drove them to the station, where trains of empty freight cars were waiting on the sidings. They were driven there under guard—by the militia and the GPU—like murderers: grandfathers and grandmothers, women and children, but no fathers, for the fathers had already been taken away in the winter. And people whispered: "They are driving off the kulaks." Just as if they were wolves. And people even shouted: "Curses on you!" But the prisoners had already stopped weeping. They had become like stone.

I myself did not see how they took them away in the trains. But I heard from others. Some of our people, for instance, went to visit them way beyond the Urals, so as to save their own lives during the famine that came later. I myself got a letter from a girl friend. And some of the so-called "kulaks" escaped from their special resettlement areas. I spoke with two of them.

They were transported in sealed freight cars, and their belongings were transported separately. They took with them only the food they had in their hands. And at a particular transit station, my girl friend wrote, they put the fathers of the families on the train. And that day there was a great gladness and weeping in those cars. They were en route more than a month. The railways were full of trainloads of similar peasants. Peasants were being transported from all over Russia. They were all tightly packed. There were no berths in the cattle cars. Those ill died en route. But they did get fed. At the main stations along the way they were given a pail of gruel and about seven ounces of bread per person.

The guard consisted of military units. The guards were not vicious. They merely treated them like cattle, and that was that. That is what my friend wrote.

And I was told by those who escaped what it was like when they got there. The provincial authorities scattered them in the Siberian taiga. Wherever a small village was nearby, the ailing and handicapped were put into huts as crowded as the prisoner-transport trains. And where there was no village nearby, they were simply set down right there on the snow. The weakest died. And those able to work began to cut down timber and didn't bother to take out the stumps. They hauled out the tree trunks and built shacks, lean-tos, makeshift sheds and dwellings. They worked almost without sleeping so that their families would not freeze to death. Only afterward did they begin to build real log cabins with two rooms, one room to a family. They "puttied" them together with moss to make them warm in the winter.

Those able to work bought timber tracts from the NKVD and got equipment from the lumber enterprises and rations for their dependents. Their settlements were called "labor settlements," and they had a commandant and foremen over them. They were paid, they told me, the same as local workers, but their entire pay was kept in special accounts. Our men are strong, and soon they began to earn more than the local people. But they did not have the right to leave their settlements or their logging area. Later on, during the war, I heard they were permitted to move about freely within their own administrative districts. And after the war, heroes of labor were given permission to move about freely even outside the immediate district. Some were even allowed to have passports, which meant they were able to travel.

My girl friend wrote me that they began to found special colonies consisting of kulaks who couldn't do ordinary work—to make them self-supporting. They were given seed on loan and got a ration from the NKVD till their first harvest. And they had a commandant and guards, just as in the labor settlements. Later on they were organized into artels, and, in addition to the commandant, they had their own elected elders.

Meanwhile back at home our new life began without the so-called "kulaks." They started to force people to join the collective farms. Meetings were under way from morning on. There were shouts and curses. Some of them shouted: "We will not join!" Others shouted: "All right, we will join, but we are not going to give up our cows." Stalin's famous essay on "dizziness from success" appeared. There was a mess all over again: they roared that Stalin had promised he would not allow them to be herded forcibly into collective farms. They wrote their declarations on the margins of newspapers: "I am leaving the collective farm to become an independent farmer." And again the officials began to drive them into the collective farms. And all the things that the so-called "kulaks" had left behind were for the most part simply stolen.

And we thought, fools that we were, that there could be no fate worse than that of the kulaks. How wrong we were! The ax fell upon the peasants right where they stood, on large and small alike. The execution by famine had arrived. By this time I no longer washed floors but was a bookkeeper instead. And, as a Party activist, I was sent to the Ukraine in order to strengthen a collective farm. In the Ukraine, we were told, they had an instinct for private property that was stronger than in the Russian Republic. And truly, truly, the whole business was much worse in the Ukraine than it was with us. I was not sent very far—we were, after all, on the very edge of the Ukraine, not more than three hours' journey from the village to which I was sent. The place was beautiful. And so I arrived there, and the people there were like everyone else. And I became the bookkeeper in the administrative office.

It seems to me that I saw and learned about everything that went on. It was not for nothing that the old man had called me a "minister"—I tell this only to you, exactly as I myself remember it, because I never brag about myself to an outsider. I kept all the accounts in my head, memorized them. And when commands came, and our troika went into session, and the leaders got drunk on vodka, I heard everything that was said.

How was it? After the liquidation of the kulaks the amount of land under cultivation dropped very sharply and so did the crop yield. But meanwhile people continued to report that without the kulaks our whole life was flourishing. The village soviet lied to the district, and the district lied to the province, and the province lied to Moscow. Everything was apparently in order, so Moscow assigned grain production and delivery quotas to the provinces, and the provinces then assigned them to the districts. And our village was given a quota that it couldn't have fulfilled in ten years! In the village soviet even those who weren't drinkers took to drink out of terror. It was clear that Moscow was basing its hopes on the Ukraine. And the upshot of it was that most of the subsequent anger was directed against the Ukraine. What they said was simple: you have failed to fulfill the plan, and that means that you yourself are an unliquidated kulak.

Of course, the grain deliveries could not be fulfilled. Smaller areas had been sown, and the crop yield on those smaller areas had shrunk. So where could it come from, that promised ocean of grain from the collective farms? The conclusion reached up top was that the grain had all been concealed, hidden away. By kulaks who had not yet been liquidated, by loafers! The "kulaks" had been removed, but the "kulak" spirit remained. Private property was master over the mind of the Ukrainian peasant.

Who was it who then signed the act which imposed mass murder? I often wonder whether it was really Stalin. I think there has never been such a decree in all the long history of Russia. Not the czars certainly, not the Tatars, nor even the German occupation forces had ever promulgated such a terrible decree. For the decree required that the peasants of the Ukraine, the Don, and the Kuban be put to death by starvation, put to death along with their tiny children. The instructions were to take away the entire seed fund. Grain was searched for as if it were not grain but bombs and machine guns. The whole earth was stabbed with bayonets and ramrods. Cellars were dug up, floors were broken through, and vegetable gardens were turned over. From some they confiscated even the grain in their houses—in pots or troughs. They even took baked bread away from one woman, loaded it onto the cart, and hauled it off to the district. Day and night the carts creaked along, laden with the confiscated grain, and dust hung over the earth. And there were no grain elevators to accommodate it, and they simply dumped it out on the earth and set guards around it. By winter the grain had been soaked by the rains and began to ferment—the Soviet government didn't even have enough canvas to cover it up!

And while they kept on hauling grain from the villages, the dust rose everywhere and one had the illusion that smoke was hovering in the air, over everything. One peasant went out of his mind and kept shouting and screaming: "Heaven is burning, the earth is burning!" He just kept on screaming and screaming. No, it was not heaven that was burning, but life itself.

So then I understood: the most important thing for the Soviet government was the plan! Fulfill the plan! Pay up your assessment, make your assigned deliveries! The state comes first, and people are a big zero.

Fathers and mothers wanted to save their children and hid a tiny bit of grain, and they were told: "You hate the country of socialism. You are trying to make the plan fail, you parasites, you pro-kulaks, you rats." They tried to answer, but it was to no avail: "We aren't trying to sabotage the plan. All we want is to feed our children and to save ourselves. After all, everyone has to eat."

I can tell you the story, but stories are words—and what this was about was life, torture, death from starvation. Incidentally, when the grain was taken away, the Party activists were told the peasants would be fed from the state grain fund. But it was not true. Not one single kernel of grain was given to the starving.

Who confiscated the grain? For the most part, local people: the Workers and Peasants Inspection officials, the district Party committee, the Komsomol, local people, and, of course, the militia, the NKVD; and in certain localities army units were used as well. I saw only one man from Moscow who had been mobilized by the Party and sent out to assist collectivization, but he didn't try very hard; instead, he kept trying to get away and go home. And again, as in the campaign to liquidate the kulaks, people became dazed, stunned, beastlike.

Grisha Sayenko, a militiaman, was married to a local village girl, and he came to the village to celebrate a holiday. He was gay, and he danced the tango and waltz and sang Ukrainian village songs. And one of the old, gray-haired men went up to him and said: "Grisha, you are making us all paupers and that's worse than murder. Why is the Workers and Peasants Government going against the peasantry, doing things the czar wouldn't do?" Grisha pushed him in the face and then went to the well to wash his hands, and he said to those who were there: "How will I be able to pick up a spoon with the hand that touched that parasite's face?"

And the dust kept rising day and night while they were hauling away the grain. The moon hung halfway up the sky like a stone, and beneath that moon everything seemed fierce and wild, and it was as hot at night as though one lay under sheepskins and the field was trampled over in all directions like an execution ground.

And people became confused, and the cattle, too, became wild and kept lowing and mooing plaintively in their fright, and the dogs howled loudly at night. And the earth crackled.

And autumn came without any rain, and the winter was a snowy winter. And there was no grain to eat. No bread.

It could not be bought in the district center because rationing was in effect. And it could not be bought at the railway stations either, in booths or kiosks. A military guard refused to let anyone near. Nor was bread being sold in nonrationed, "commercial" stores.

With the autumn people began to use up their potatoes, and, since there was no bread, they disappeared very quickly. By Christmas they began to slaughter their cattle. The cattle were by then mostly skin and bones anyway, and the meat was stringy and tough. Then, of course, they killed the chickens. All the meat went swiftly. Not a drop of milk was to be had. Not an egg was left in the village either. But the worst thing was that there was no grain, no bread. They had taken every last kernel of grain from the village. There was no seed to be sown for spring wheat or other spring grains. The entire seed fund had been confiscated. The only hope was in the winter grains, but the winter grains were still under the snow. The spring was far away. And the villagers were already starving. They had eaten their meat, and whatever millet they had left; they were eating the last of their potatoes, and in the case of the larger families the potatoes were already gone.

Everyone was in terror. Mothers looked at their children and began to scream in fear. They screamed as if a snake had crept into their house. And this snake was famine, starvation, death. What was to be done? The peasants had one thing only on their minds—something to eat. They would suck, move their jaws, and the saliva would flow and they would keep swallowing it down, but it wasn't food. At night, one would wake up, and all around was silence. Not a conversation anywhere. Not an accordion either. Like the grave. Only famine was on the move. Only famine did not sleep. The children would cry from morning on, asking for bread. And what could their mothers give them—snow? And there was no help. The Party officials had one answer to all entreaties: "You should have worked harder; you shouldn't have loafed." And then they would also say: "Look about your village; you've got enough buried there to last you three years."

Yet in the winter there was still no real honest-to-God starvation. Of course, people became weak. Stomachs puffed up somewhat from potato peelings, but there was no real swelling as yet. They began to dig up acorns from beneath the snow and dried them out, and the miller set his stones wider apart and they ground the acorns up for flour. They baked bread from the acorns—more properly, pancakes. They were very dark, darker even then rye bread. Some people added bran to them or ground-up potato peelings. But the acorns were quickly used up because the oak forest was not a large one and three villages rushed to it all at once. Meanwhile a Party representative came from the city and said at the village soviet: "There you see, look at the parasites! They went digging for acorns in the snow with their bare hands—they'll do anything to get out of working."

At school the upper grades continued to attend classes until nearly spring. But the lower grades stopped during the winter. And in the spring the school shut down. The teacher went off to the city. And the medical assistant left too. He had nothing to eat. Anyway, you can't cure starvation with medicines. And all the various representatives stopped coming from the city too. Why come? There was nothing to be had from the starving. There was no use coming any more. No use providing them with medical help and no use teaching them anything either. Once things reached the point where the state could not squeeze anything more out of the human being, he became useless. Why teach him? Why cure him?

The starving people were left to themselves. The state had abandoned them. In the villages people went from house to house, begging from each other. The poor begged from the poor, the starving begged from the starving. Whoever had fewer children or none might have something left by spring. And those with many children kept begging from them. And occasionally they were given a handful of bran or a couple of potatoes. But the Party members gave nothing. Not out of greed, nor because of viciousness. They were just very afraid. And the state gave not one tiny kernel to the starving. Though it was on the grain of the peasants that the state was founded, that it stood. Could Stalin not know what was happening? Old people recalled what the famine had been like under Czar Nicholas. They had been helped then. They had been lent food. The peasants went to the cities to beg "in the name of Christ." Soup kitchens were opened to feed them, and students collected donations. And here, under the government of workers and peasants, not even one kernel of grain was given them. There were blockades along all the highways, where militia, NKVD men, troops were stationed; the starving people were not to be allowed into the cities. Guards surrounded all the railroad stations. There were guards at even the tiniest of whistle stops. No bread for you, breadwinners! And in the cities the workers were given eight hundred grams—a pound and a half—of bread each day. Good Lord, could that even be imagined—eight hundred grams! And the peasant children in the villages got not one gram. That is exactly how the Nazis put the Jewish children into the Nazi gas chambers: "You are not allowed to live, you are all Jews!" And it was impossible to understand, grasp, comprehend For these children were

Soviet children, and those who were putting them to death were Soviet people. These children were Russians, and those who were putting them to death were Russians. And the government was a government of workers and peasants. Why this massacre?

It was when the snow began to melt that the village was up to its neck in real starvation.

The children kept crying and crying. They did not sleep. And they began to ask for bread at night too. People's faces looked like clay. Their eyes were dull and drunken. They went about as though asleep. They inched forward, feeling their way one foot at a time, and they supported themselves by keeping one hand against the wall. They began to move around less. Starvation made them totter. They moved less and less, and they spent more time lying down. And they kept thinking they heard the creaking of a cart bringing flour, sent to them by Stalin from the district center so as to save the children.

The women turned out to be stronger and more enduring than the men. They had a tighter hold on life. And they had more to suffer from it too. For the children kept asking their mothers for something to eat. Some of the women would talk to their children and try to explain and kiss them: "Don't cry. Be patient. Where can I get anything?" Others became almost insane: "Stop whining, or I'll kill you!" And then they would beat the children with whatever was at hand just to put an end to their crying and begging. And some of them ran away from their homes and went to their neighbors' houses, so as not to hear their children cry.

No dogs and cats were left. They had been slaughtered. And it was hard to catch them too. The animals had become afraid of people and their eyes were wild. People boiled them. All there was were tough veins and muscles. And from their heads they made a meat jelly.

The snow melted and people began to swell up. The edema of starvation had begun. Faces were swollen, legs swollen like pillows; water bloated their stomachs; people kept urinating all the time. Often they couldn't even make it out of the house. And the peasant children! Have you ever seen the newspaper photographs of the children in the German camps? They were just like that: their heads like heavy balls on thin little necks, like storks, and one could see each bone of their arms and legs protruding from beneath the skin, how bones joined, and the entire skeleton was stretched over with skin that was like yellow gauze. And the children's faces were aged, tormented, just as if they were seventy years old. And by spring they no longer had faces at all. Instead, they had birdlike heads with beaks, or frog heads—thin, wide lips—and some of them resembled fish, mouths open. Not human faces. And the eyes. Oh, Lord! Comrade Stalin, good God, did you see those eyes? Perhaps, in fact, he did not know. After all, he was the one who wrote the essay on "dizziness from success."

And now they ate anything at all. They caught mice, rats, snakes, sparrows, ants, earthworms. They ground up bones into flour, and did the same with leather and shoe soles; they cut up old skins and furs to make noodles of a kind, and they cooked glue. And when the grass came up, they began to dig up the roots and eat the leaves and the buds; they used everything there was: dandelions, and burdocks, and bluebells, and willowroot, and sedums, and nettles and every other kind of edible grass and root and herb they could find. They dried out linden leaves and ground them into flour—but there were too few linden in our region.

The pancakes made from the linden leaves were greenish in color and worse than those made of acorn flour.

And no help came! And they no longer asked for any. Even now when I start thinking about it all, I begin to go out of my mind. How could Stalin have turned his back on human beings? He went to such lengths as this horrible massacre! After all, Stalin had bread. He had food to eat. What it adds up to is that he intentionally, deliberately, killed people by starvation. He refused to help even the children. And that makes Stalin worse than Herod. How can it be, I keep thinking to myself, that he took their grain and bread away, and then killed people by starvation? Such things are simply unimaginable! But then I think and remember: it did take place, it did take place! Then again I think that it simply could not really have happened.

Before they had completely lost their strength, the peasants went on foot across country to the railroad. Not to the stations where the guards kept them away, but to the tracks. And when the Kiev-Odessa express came past, they would just kneel there and cry: "Bread, bread!" They would lift up their horrible starving children for people to see. And sometimes people would throw them pieces of bread and other scraps. The train would thunder on past, and the dust would settle down, and the whole village would be there crawling along the tracks, looking for crusts. But an order was issued that whenever trains were traveling through the famine provinces the guards were to shut the windows and pull down the curtains. Passengers were not allowed at the windows. Yes, and in the end the peasants themselves stopped going to the railroads. They had too little strength left to get to the tracks—in fact, they didn't have enough strength to crawl out of their huts and into the yard.

I can still recall how one old man brought the farm chairman a piece of newspaper he had found near the tracks. There was an item in it about a Frenchman, a famous minister, who had been taken to Dnepropetrovsk Province where the famine was at its worst, even worse than ours. People had become cannibals there, but his hosts had taken him to a local village, to a collective farm nursery school, and he had asked them: "What did you have for lunch today?" And the children answered, "Chicken soup with *pirozhki* and rice cutlets." I read it myself and I can still see that piece of newspaper right now. What did it mean? It meant that they were killing millions and keeping the whole thing quiet, deceiving the whole world! Chicken soup! Cutlets! And on our farm they had eaten all the earthworms. And the old man said to the farm chairman: "When Nicholas was Czar, the whole world wrote about the famine and was urged to give: 'Help, help! The peasantry is dying.' And you Herods, you child-killers, are showing off Potemkin villages, making theater out of it!"

The village moaned as it foresaw its approaching death. The whole village moaned—not out of logic, but from the soul, as leaves moan in the wind or straw crackles. And I myself saw red; why were they moaning so plaintively? One had to be made of stone to hear all that moaning and at the same time eat one's own ration of bread. I used to go outdoors with my bread ration and I could hear them moaning. I would go farther, and then it would seem as if they had fallen silent. And then I would go on a little farther, and it would begin again. At that point, it was the next village down the line. And it seemed as if the whole earth were groaning, together with the people on it. There was no God. Who could hear them?

One of the NKVD men said to me: "Do you know what they call your villages in the provincial center? A hard-school cemetery." But when I first heard those words, I did not understand them.

And how wonderful the weather was! At the beginning of summer there were rains, quick-falling, light, and the hot sun mingled with the rain, and as a result the lush wheat stood there like a wall. You could cut it with an ax, it was so strong and good. And it was high, taller than a man. And I saw so many rainbows that summer, and thundershowers and warm rain.

That whole winter they had wondered whether there would be a harvest. They had asked the old men what they thought, and they searched for good omens. Their whole hope was in the winter wheat. And their hopes were justified, but they were too weak to harvest it. I went into a hut. People lay there, barely breathing, or else not breathing at all, some of them on the bed and others on the stove, and the daughter of the owner, whom I knew, lay on the floor in some kind of insane fit, gnawing on the leg of the stool. It was horrible. When she heard me come in, she did not turn around but growled, just as a dog growls if you come near when he is gnawing on a bone.

Deaths from starvation mowed down the village. First the children, then the old people, then those of middle age. At first they dug graves and buried them, and then as things got worse they stopped. Dead people lay there in the yards, and in the end they remained right in their huts. Things fell silent. The whole village died. Who died last I do not know.

Those of us who worked in the collective farm administration were taken off to the city.

First I went to Kiev. At that time they had begun to sell unrationed bread at high prices in the "commercial" stores, as they were called. You should have seen what went on! The lines were half a kilometer in length the night before the stores even opened. As you know yourself, there are all kinds of queues. In some of them people stand and smile and laugh and eat sunflower seeds. And in others people write down their number in the line on a piece of paper. And in a third kind, the kind in which people do not laugh or joke, they write their number in chalk either on the palm or the back of their hand. But these lines were of a special kind. I have never ever seen any like them. People held onto the belts of those ahead and clung for dear life. If one person stumbled, the whole line would shake and quaver as if a wave had passed along it. It was as if a dance had begun—from side to side. All of them staggered heavily. They were terrified of being unable to keep hold of the person in front, of their hands slipping, and losing their place. And the women began to scream out of fear. And the whole long queue howled, and it seemed as if some of them had gone out of their minds—they kept singing and dancing. Now and then, some young hoodlums would break into the line. They would look for the places where the links in the chain were weakest. And when the hoodlums came near, everyone would start to howl again with fear—it seemed as though they were singing. They were city people standing there in line for unrationed "commercial" bread—deprived people, non-Party people, craftsmen—or else people from the suburbs. Many of them were people who had been refused ration cards.

And the peasants kept crawling from the village into the city. All the stations were surrounded by guards. All the trains were searched. Everywhere along the roads were roadblocks—troops, NKVD. Yet despite all this the peasants made their way into Kiev. They would crawl through the fields, through empty lots, through the swamps, through the woods—anywhere to bypass the roadblocks set up for them. They were unable to walk; all they could do was crawl. People hurried about on their affairs, some going to work, some to the movies, and the streetcars were running—and there were the starving children, old men, girls, crawling about among them on all fours. They were like mangy dogs and cats of some kind. And they had the nerve to want to be treated like human beings! They were modest. A young girl would crawl along, swollen up, looking like an ape; she would whine, but she would pull down her skirt and hide her hair beneath her kerchief. She was a peasant girl, and this was the first time she had come to Kiev. But the ones who had managed to crawl their way there were the more fortunate, one out of ten thousand. And even when they got there, they found no salvation. They lay starving on the ground, and they spluttered and begged but were unable to eat. A crust might lie right next to them, but they couldn't see it, and they lay dying.

In the mornings horses pulled flattop carts through the city, and the corpses of those who had died in the night were collected. I saw one such flattop cart with children lying on it. They were just as I have described them, thin, elongated faces, like those of dead birds, with sharp beaks. These tiny birds had flown into Kiev and what good had it done them? Some of them were still muttering, and their heads were still turning. I asked the driver about them, and he just waved his hands and said: "By the time they get where they are being taken they will be silent too."

I saw one young girl crawl across the sidewalk; a janitor kicked her, and she slid into the street. She didn't even look back. She just kept crawling along swiftly, trying to find the strength to go on. She brushed off her dress, too, where it had gotten dusty. I bought a Moscow paper that very same day and read an article by Maxim Gorky in which he said that children needed cultural toys. Are we to suppose that Maxim Gorky did not know about those children being hauled off on a flattop cart drawn by dray horses? What kind of toys did they need? But perhaps he did know, too, for that matter. And perhaps he, too, kept silent, like all the rest. And perhaps he, too, wrote, as others had written, that those dead children were eating chicken soup. The very same drayman told me that the greatest number of corpses were near the unrationed "commercial" bread stores. A swollen, starving person would eat a crust and it would finish him off. I can still remember the Kiev of those days, even though I spent only three days there in all.

And this is what I came to understand. In the beginning, starvation drives a person out of his house. In its first stage, he is tormented and driven as though by fire and torn both in the guts and in the soul. And so he tries to escape his home. People dig up worms, collect grass, and even make the effort to break through and get to the city. Away from home, away from home! And then a day comes when the starving person crawls back into his house. And the meaning of this is that famine, starvation, has won. The human being cannot be saved. He lies down on his bed and stays there. Not just because he has no strength, but because he has no interest in life and no longer cares about living. He lies there quite quietly and does not want to be touched. And he does not even want to eat. He keeps urinating constantly and he has continuous runs and he becomes sleepy. All he wants is to be left alone, and for things to be quiet. Starving men lie there dying. And I have heard the same from P.O.W.'s too. If the P.O.W. lay down on his bunk and did not try to get up and get his ration, it meant he would soon die.

Some went insane. They never did become completely still. One could tell from their eyes—because their eyes shone. These were the people who cut up and cooked corpses, who killed their own children and ate them. In them the beast rose to the top as the human being died. I saw one. She had been brought to the district center under convoy. Her face was human, but her eyes were those of a wolf. These are cannibals, they said, and must all be shot. But they themselves, who drove the mother to the madness of eating her own children, are evidently not guilty at all! For that matter, can you really find anyone who is guilty? Just go and ask, and they will all tell you that they did it for the sake of virtue, for everybody's good. That's why they drove mothers to cannibalism!

It was then that I saw for myself that every starving person is like a cannibal. He is consuming his own flesh, leaving only his bones intact. He devours his fat to the last droplet. And then his mind grows dim, because he has consumed his own mind. In the end the starving man has devoured himself completely.

I thought, too, that every starving person dies in his own particular way. In one hut there would be something like a war. Everyone would keep close watch over everyone else. People would take crumbs from each other. The wife turned against her husband and the husband against his wife. The mother hated the children. And in some other hut love would be inviolable to the very last. I knew one woman with four children. She would tell them fairy stories and legends so that they would forget their hunger. Her own tongue could hardly move, but she would take them into her arms even though she had hardly the strength to lift her arms when they were empty. Love lived on within her. And people noticed that where there was hate people died off more swiftly. Yet love, for that matter, saved no one. The whole village perished, one and all. No life remained in it.

What I found out later was that everything fell silent in our village. The children were no more to be heard. They didn't need any cultural toys, nor any chicken soup either. They no longer moaned. There was no one left to moan. I found out that troops were sent in to harvest the winter wheat. The army men were not allowed to enter the village, however. They were quartered in their tents. They were told there had been an epidemic. But they kept complaining that a horrible stink was coming from the village. The troops stayed to plant the spring wheat too. And the next year new settlers were brought in from Orel Province. This was the rich Ukrainian land, the black earth, whereas the Orel peasants were accustomed to frequent harvest failures. The new settlers left their women and children in temporary shelters near the station and the men were brought into the village. They were given pitchforks and told to go through the huts and drag out the corpses. The dead men and women still lay there, some on the floor and some in their beds. The stink in the huts was still frightful. The new settlers covered their noses and mouths with kerchiefs and began to drag out the bodies, but the bodies fell apart in pieces. Then they buried the pieces outside the village. And it was then that I understood what was meant by the phrase "a hard-school cemetery." When they had removed the corpses from the huts, they brought in the womenfolk to clean the floors and to whitewash the walls. Everything was done as it was supposed to be done. But the stink remained. They whitewashed a second time, and they spread new clay on the floors, but the stink remained. They were unable either to eat or sleep in those huts, and they returned to Orel Province. But of course the land did not remain empty. It is rich land.

And now it is as though they had never lived at all. Yet many, many things took place there. There was love. And wives left husbands. And daughters were married off. And there were drunken brawls, and people came to visit, and they baked bread. And how they worked! And they sang songs. And children went to school. And a movie projector was brought in, and the people went to see the films.

And nothing was left of it at all. Where has that life gone? And what has become of all that awful torment and torture? Can it really be that nothing at all is left of it? Can it really be that no one will ever answer for everything that happened? That it will all be forgotten without even any words to commemorate it? That the grass has grown over it?

So I ask you: How can all this be?

There, you see how our night has passed, that it is already dawn and growing light. It is time for both of us to pull ourselves together and go to work.

15

Vasily Timofeyevich had a soft voice and his gestures were somehow quiet, hesitating, gentle. And when he and Hanna talked together, her black eyes lowered their gaze, and she would answer him in a barely audible voice.

After their marriage they became even more shy and retiring than they had been before. He was a man of sixty, whom the neighborhood children called "grandfather." And he was really very shy, very embarrassed, that he had married a young girl even though he was gray-haired, somewhat balding, and wrinkled, and that he was happy in his love, and that when he looked upon her he would whisper: "My dear darling . . . my sweetheart." Once upon a time, as a slip of a girl, she had imagined what her future husband would be like. He would be a Civil War Hero like Shchors, and the best accordion-player in the village, and he would write heartfelt verses like Taras Shchevchenko. But her gentle heart nonetheless understood the strength of the love Vasily Timofeyevich bore her, that unlucky, poor, shy, elderly man who had always lived someone else's life and never his own. And he could understand and appreciate her youthful hope too. A peasant cavalier would suddenly appear and take her away from her father's crowded hut. But here was Vasily Timofeyevich, who had come for her in old boots, with the big dark hands of a peasant, coughing in a guilty sort of way, and gazing upon her with admiration, with happiness, with guilt, with grief. And she, too, felt guilty in his presence and was meek and silent.

And their son, Grisha, was a quiet child. He never cried.

His mother, who was still like a thin slip of a girl after he was born, sometimes went up to the cradle at night and, seeing the boy lying there with open eyes, she would say: "You should at least cry a little, Grishenka. Why are you always silent, silent and still?"

In their hut the wife and the husband spoke in soft voices and their neighbors were astonished. "Why do you speak so quietly?"

It was strange that she, a young woman, and he, an elderly, homely peasant, were very much alike in meekness of heart, gentleness, shyness.

They both worked without letup, and they even hesitated to raise their voices when their brigadier drove them out to work in the fields unfairly and out of turn.

On one occasion Vasily Timofeyevich rode to the district center with the collective farm chairman on an errand for the collective farm stable. While the chairman went about his business at the district offices for agriculture, finance, and such, he, after tying the horses to a hitching post, went to the district store and bought his wife a present—poppyseed cakes, sugar candies, ring-shaped crackers, and nuts, a little of each, maybe five ounces. And when he entered their hut and untied his white kerchief, his wife held up her hands and clapped them joyously, and cried: "Oh, oh!" And Vasily Timofeyevich went off into the passageway, shyly, so that she would not see the tears in his happy eyes.

She embroidered a shirt for him. And she never ever did know that Vasily Timofeyevich Karpenko hardly slept all night long and kept going barefooted up to the chest of drawers on which the shirt still lay, and stroked it with his hand, his fingers feeling the cross-stitch of the simply embroidered design. When he brought his wife home from the maternity ward of the district hospital, and she held her child in her arms, it seemed to him that if he were to live a thousand years he would never forget that day.

Sometimes he was simply overcome with dismay: how could it possibly be that such happiness had come into his life? How could it possibly be that he could wake in the middle of the night and listen to the breathing of his wife and his son?

And this is how it went. He came home from work and he saw the diaper drying on the wattle fence and the smoke rising from his chimney. He looked upon his wife—she was bent down over the cradle. Then she was putting a plate of borsch on the table and smiling about something. He looked at her hands, at her hair escaping a little from beneath her kerchief. He listened to her gossip. Sometimes, briefly, she went out into the passageway, and he felt pangs of loneliness; his heart ached while he waited for her, and when she returned, he was overjoyed. And she, catching his glance, smiled at him meekly and sadly.

Vasily Timofeyevich was the first to die. He was two days ahead of tiny Grisha. He had given nearly all the crumbs he had to his wife and child, and that is why he died before they did. In all likelihood, there was no self-sacrifice in the whole world greater than his and no desperation greater than the desperation he suffered as he looked upon his wife, disfigured by the swelling dropsy of starvation, and upon his dying son.

He felt no reproach or wrath against the great and meaningless thing that the state and Stalin had committed—even in his final hour. He did not even ask the question "Why?" He did not ask why the torment of death by starvation had been meted out to him and his wife, meek, obedient, submissive people, and to his quiet year-old baby boy.

The skeletons spent the winter together in their rotting rags—the husband, the wife, and the small son—smiling pallidly. They had not been parted in death.

And then in the spring when the starlings came, the representative of the agricultural section entered their hut, with his kerchief covering his nose, and he looked at the kerosene lamp without any glass, at the ikon in the corner, at the chest of drawers, at the cold frying pans there, at the bed, and he said: "In here, two adults and one small one."

The brigadier, standing there on the threshold made sacred by love and meekness, nodded his head and made a mark on a piece of paper.

When they went out into the fresh air, the representative of the agricultural department looked at the white huts, at the green orchards, and said: "Once you have removed the corpses, don't bother to try to restore all this mess."

16

At work Ivan Grigoryevich heard that bribes were given and taken in the municipal court; that one could buy one's children high marks on competitive examinations in the Radio Technical Institute; that a factory director would, for a bribe, supply scarce metal to artels producing consumer goods; that a mill manager had built himself a two-story house on stolen money and had had floors laid with oak parquet; that the chief of the militia had released from custody a famous bigwig jeweler in return for the huge bribe of 600,000 rubles, paid by the jeweler's relatives; and that even the political boss of the whole city, the first secretary of the city Party committee, was willing—in return for under-the-table compensation—to order the chairman of the city soviet to make available to his benefactor an apartment in a choice new apartment house on the main street.

The employees in the artel for the handicapped had been excited all morning. Everyone had heard about the decision just in from the provincial capital on the case against the stockroom chief of the city's richest artel, "Mekhposhiv." This artel manufactured fur coats, women's coats, and reindeer and karakul hats. And even though the principal defendant in the case was the modest stockroom chief, the case was spectacular. Like a centipede, it had wormed its way into the whole life of a large city. The decision had been awaited a long time, and there had been frequent arguments about it during lunch breaks. Some said that "the investigator for particularly important cases," who had come from Moscow to the provincial capital, would have no qualms about exposing the involvement of the city Party leadership in this big case.

After all, even children knew that the city prosecutor went driving about in a Volga limousine that the balding stammerer of a stockroom chief had presented to him as a gift; that the secretary of the city Party committee had brought back from Riga furniture given him by the stockroom chief—complete suites for dining room and bedroom; that the wife of the chief of the militia had been sent off to Adler, to spend two months on holiday in the Sanatorium of the Council of Ministers—all at the expense of the stockroom chief—and that on the day she left she had been presented with an emerald ring.

Others, skeptics, said that the Muscovite would not be so brash as to involve the bosses of the city and that the whole weight of the blow would have to be borne by the stockroom chief and the administration of the artel.

Then the son of the stockroom chief, a university student who had just flown in from the provincial capital, brought the wholly unexpected news that "the investigator for particularly important cases" had quashed the whole case for lack of evidence. The stockroom chief had been released, and the personal guarantee not to leave the area exacted from the artel chairman and two of his artel members had been rescinded.

For some reason the decision of the plenipotentiary Moscow jurist amused all the people in the artel—skeptics and optimists. During their lunch break the handicapped ate bread, sausage, tomatoes, cucumbers, and laughed and joked; they were overjoyed by the human weakness of "the investigator for particularly important cases." They were amused by the omnipotence of that balding stammerer of a stockroom chief.

As for Ivan Grigoryevich, he thought about the fact that the path first trod by men who had taken an oath of poverty, by barefoot apostles, by fanatics of the communes, had led in the end, and not by any means as an accident, to people completely prepared to go to any length, to engage in any kind of swindle, for the sake of their rich country houses, for the sake of their private automobiles, for the sake of a big piggy bank with lots of money inside.

One night, after work, Ivan Grigoryevich went to the office of the physician at the polyclinic whose name he had heard from Anna Sergeyevna. The physician, who had finished seeing patients, was taking off his white coat.

"I would like to know, Doctor, about the health of Anna Sergeyevna Mikhalyeva."

"Are you her husband, her father?" asked the doctor.

"No, I am not a relative. But she is a person who is very close to me."

"So that's how it is," said the doctor. "Well, why not? I will tell you. She has lung cancer. There's no help for her either through surgery or in a health resort."

17

Three weeks passed and Anna Sergeyevna was put in a hospital.

As they said good-bye, Anna Sergeyevna told Ivan Grigoryevich: "Obviously it is not our fate to be happy in this world."

That same day, when Ivan Grigoryevich was not at home, Anna Sergeyevna's sister came and took Alyesha back to the village.

Ivan Grigoryevich returned to an empty room. Everything was quiet. And it seemed to him that although he had lived all his life alone and lonely, not until that evening had he really felt loneliness in all its force.

That night he did not sleep. He kept thinking, "It is not our fate . . ."

Only his distant childhood seemed to him bright and joyous.

And now that happiness had looked him in the eyes, had breathed upon him, he measured with all possible sensitivity the life he had led.

Great indeed was the pain of realizing that he was helpless to save Anna Sergeyevna, or ease the terminal torment which awaited her. And strangely, he seemed to find comfort for his grief in thinking of the decades he had suffered and survived in camps and prisons.

He thought of them as he tried to comprehend the truth, the justice, of Russian life, the tie between the past and the present.

He hoped Anna Sergeyevna would come home from the hospital, and that he would have the chance to tell her everything he had worked out, everything he had recollected.

She would share with him the burden and the clarity of his recollection. Therein lay the comfort for his grief; in this his love consisted.

18

Ivan Grigoryevich often thought about his months in the Lubyanka and later in the Butyrka. He had been in the Butyrka three times, but it was the summer of 1937 that he remembered most vividly. At the time, of course, he had been befogged, half-insane. And it had taken all these years for the fog to disappear, for everything to begin to come clear.

The cells were unimaginably overcrowded in 1937—a hundred prisoners jammed into space intended for ten. They lay on the board bunks, piled right up against each other, sweat-drenched in the sultry heat of July and August, able to turn over only in unison on the monitor's orders—he was the former commander of a cavalry division. To get to the latrine barrel one had to step over bodies. And the newcomers were sleeping next to it, wherefore they had been christened "parachutists." In that crowded closeness sleep was like delirium.

The very walls of the prison seemed to quiver from the internal pressure, like a steam boiler. The Butyrka hummed all night long. Cars roared into the courtyard delivering newly arrested prisoners, pale as death, who stared about them at the prison kingdom. Black Marias kept roaring out with loads of prisoners: for interrogation at the Lubyanka, for torture at Lefortovo, for transport assignment at Krasnaya Presnya, or to be loaded directly on transports to Siberia. To those who were leaving for good, the guards shouted: "With your things!" And their comrades bade them farewell.

Along brightly lit corridors, prisoners' feet shuffled, and guards' weapons clanked. In the corridor walls were enclosed niches called "boxes," into which a prisoner would at times be shoved hastily—to wait there in the dark until another prisoner accompanied by another guard had passed.

Cell windows were shuttered with thick wooden panels so that light seeped only through narrow slits. The prisoners told time not by the sun and stars but by the prison schedule. Bright electric lights burned mercilessly night and day, and the prisoners blamed them for the heat and the close air. Ventilators hummed constantly, but the air from the asphalt-paved out-of-doors brought no relief in July. All night the air clung like pads of felt to lungs and head.

Close to dawn prisoners were brought back from interrogation. Some collapsed exhausted on their board bunks. Some sobbed and groaned. Some sat there frozen, big eyes staring straight ahead. Others rubbed their swollen legs and poured out the story of what they had undergone. Some couldn't make it on their own, and were dragged in by the guards. Some who had undergone continuous interrogation for days on end were taken on stretchers directly to the prison hospital. But this stinking, fetid cell was, to a man being worked over in the interrogator's chambers, a sweet and lovely vision, a dream. He longed to return to the dear tortured faces of his cellmates.

And these prisoners of 1937—all these government and Party officials, military officers, intellectuals, the erstwhile possessors of rank, power, perquisites, fame—represented the full spectrum of the men raised to great heights by the Revolution. Men of all nationalities, from all walks of life, they had joined the Revolution, fought in the Civil War, and poured from the boondocks into all the various institutions and organizations set up to be the executive arms of the Revolution. A new state was being created, of a kind never before seen in history. Sacrifice, cruelty, deprivation, loss of life meant nothing. These were necessary acts, undertaken in the name of Russia and of all laboring humanity, of the working people.

Came the thirties and all those young men who had fought in the Civil War had turned into graying forty-year-olds, sitting in offices equipped with telephones and secretaries, wearing jackets and ties instead of field shirts, going about in autos. They had acquired a taste for good wines, for spas like Kislovodsk, for famous doctors. Yet in their eyes the era of the Revolution, of the Committees of the Poor, of the First and Second Comintern Congresses, remained their finest hour. They looked back to the high-peaked Budyenny helmets, leather jackets, millet porridge, torn boots, and such earth-shattering ideas as the "World Commune" as the high point of their lives. And it was not for their automobiles and country houses that they had built the new state, but for the Revolution. It was for the Revolution and the New Russia that sacrifices had been exacted, cruelties committed, and blood shed.

This was the generation which vanished in the great purge from 1936 to 1939—and it was not, of course, monolithic.

The first to feel the blow were the fanatics, the wreckers of the old world. Their emotions, devotion, fanaticism rose from their hatred for enemies of the Revolution. They hated everyone and everything hostile to the Revolution—the whole spectrum of political opposition inside and outside Russia.

They destroyed the old world and thirsted for the new—but they themselves did not build it. These people, paradoxically, who shed so much blood and who hated with such passion, were in their hearts childishly good-natured. They were fanatics, mad men perhaps, who hated for the sake of love. They were the dynamite the Party used to blow up the old Russia, to clear the site for the excavations where the foundations of the great new structure would be laid, built with the granite of the new state.

With them came the first of the new builders—whose efforts were devoted to setting up a Party and government apparatus, to building factories, mills, mines, railways, highways, digging canals, the mechanization of agriculture. These were the earliest Red businessmen, the fathers of Soviet pig iron, calico, aircraft. In defiance of normal work schedules, Siberian cold, the heat of the Kara-Kum Desert, these men dug the foundations and raised the walls of the Soviet skyscrapers. Gvakhariya, Frankfurt, Zavenyagin, Gugel . . . and the rest. Only a few of them died natural deaths.

Beside them were the Party leaders, the creators and governors of the new Soviet national republics, territories, provinces—Postyshev, Kirov, Vareikis, Betal Kalmykov,

Faizula Khodzhayev, Mendel Khatayevich, Eikhe . . . and the rest. And not one of them died a natural death.

They were vivid people—orators, authors, connoisseurs of philosophy, lovers of poetry, hunters, carousers. Their phones rang all hours of the day and night. Their secretaries worked in three shifts. But, unlike the fanatics and dreamers, they knew how to relax, how to enjoy expensive, sunny country houses, hunting for wild boar and mountain goat, gay Sunday luncheons that lasted many hours, Armenian cognac and Georgian wines. They no longer wore tattered coats in winter. And the gabardine of their soldierly, Stalin-like field shirts was more costly than English woolens. They were outstanding for their energy and their will—and for their complete and total inhumanity. They were all inhuman—including those who loved nature, poetry, music, or good times. They clearly understood, of course, that the new world was being built for the sake of the people. Yet they were not at all disturbed that the workers, peasants, and intelligentsia—the people—were the most difficult obstacles of all to the building of the new world.

It often seemed that these leaders of the new world were for the most part spending their enormously powerful energy, their implacable will, and their boundless cruelty in forcing people to work beyond all reason and measure—overtime, without a day off, half-starving, quartered in barracks, receiving paupers' wages, and paying taxes, levies, loans, and assessments unheard of in history.

And under these leaders human beings built things human beings had no need for—the White Sea–Baltic Canal, Arctic mines, Arctic railways, superheavy industrial installations hidden in the taiga, superpowerful hydroelectric plants in the Siberian wilderness. Often it seemed that these factories, canals, seas were as useless to the state as they were to men and women. Often it seemed as if their sole purpose was to shackle the masses in heavy labor.

Marx, Lenin, Stalin, all three, asserted the primacy of economics over politics as the first and basic truth of their revolutionary teaching. Yet the basis of the state founded by Lenin was politics, not economics. Not one of the builders of the new world ever stopped to consider that the building of those enormous factories for heavy industry, which were useless to human beings and, often, useless to the state as well, contradicted the Marxist thesis of the primacy of economics over politics. Politics determined the content of Stalin's Five-Year Plans—and his other actions and undertakings.

Those engaged in building the Soviet state and the Soviet Union came to realize, of course, that they were not carrying out a World Revolution or building a World Commune—as they had thought they were doing during the Civil War. But they did believe that socialism built in one country would result in the dawn of the world-wide socialist era.

Then came 1937. And the prisons were filled with hundreds of thousands of the generation of the Revolution and the Civil War, the fathers of the Soviet state who were at the same time its children. The prisons they had built for the enemies of the New Russia had opened their gates wide for *them*, and the avenging sword of the dictatorship they had forged now descended upon them. They could not understand. Why were confessions being extorted from them by torture; why were they proclaimed enemies of the people; why were they being cast out from the very life they had defended in battle and had built; why were they being equated with the enemies of the Revolution whom they had hated and whom they had themselves destroyed like mad dogs; why were they in the very same cells and camp barracks with the remaining Mensheviks and factory owners and estate owners from czarist times? Some were certain there had been a *coup d'état,* that the government had been seized by enemies of the Revolution, and that these enemies, having assumed the Soviet language and concepts as disguises, were destroying those who had created the Soviet state.

They were all mixed up together. One Party secretary might find himself on a cell bunk next to the Party secretary who had exposed him as an enemy of the people and replaced him, and then the even more recent Party secretary, who had exposed and replaced the second, would arrive.

There was the roar of the trains hurtling north, the howling and snarling of the police dogs, the creaking of jackboots and of the women prisoners' high-heeled shoes on the crackling taiga snow, the scratching of interrogators' pens, the screech of spades on frozen ground digging graves for those dead of scurvy or heart attacks or frozen to death.

There were the repentant speeches of those begging forgiveness at Party meetings, and white deathly-pale lips repeating after the interrogator: "I confess that having become a paid agent of a foreign intelligence service . . . etc., etc."

And inside the thick walls of the Lubyanka or the Butyrka there was the unending crackle of pistol and rifle fire—nine grams in the chest or the back of the head of those thousands of tens of thousands of innocents who had been denounced for "having committed particularly vicious terrorist and espionage acts."

And those who remained out in freedom kept waiting for the nighttime knock at the door.

In this chaotic, mad, absurd scene, amid the insanity of false charges, the generation of the Civil War departed, and new times arrived, and new people appeared on the scene.

19

Lyeva Mekler, Lev Naumovich . . . In freedom he used to wear shoes size forty-five, and a Moscow suit size fifty-eight. And his sentence was Section 58: betrayal of the Motherland, terror, diversionist activity. . . well, and some other minor details which did not matter.

They did not shoot him—probably because he was among the first to be arrested, and at that time there wasn't the lavish generosity in handing out the death sentence that came later.

He went right on, nearsighted, absent-mindedly squinting and stumbling, through all the circles of hell of prison and camp, and he did not perish because the fire of faith which had been burning within him since his adolescence had preserved him against minus-forty degrees of cold at night, against the fierce wind, dystrophy, and scurvy. He had not died even when a barge filled with prisoners had sunk in the Yenisei. He had not died even from the bloody runs.

He had not been cut to pieces by the thieves. He had not

been tortured to death in punishment cells, nor had the security operations officer beaten him to death during interrogation. And he had not been shot during the mass purge when they shot every tenth man.

Whence had that powerful flame of fanaticism flared within him, this son of a sad, sly shopkeeper from the shtetl of Fastov, this student in the commercial school who had read the books of the "Golden Library" and of Louis-Henri Boussenard? Neither he nor his father had any reason to store up within their hearts that hatred of capitalism which was fed in dark coal mines, in smoky factories.

Who had given him a fighter's soul? Was it the example of Zhelyabov and Kalyayev, or the wisdom of the *Communist Manifesto,* or the suffering of the impoverished people right beside him?

Or was it that the smoldering coals were buried deep within his thousand-year inheritance, ready to burst into flame—to do battle with Caesar's Roman soldiers, to confront the bonfires of the Spanish Inquisition, to join in the starving frenzy of the Talmudists, to emerge in the shtetl organization for self-defense during the pogroms?

Perhaps the age-old chain of humiliations, the anguish of the Babylonian exile, the humiliation of the ghetto, the impoverishment of the Pale, gave rise to, were the forge wherein was tempered, the soul of the Bolshevik Lev Mekler?

His inability to adapt to ordinary life aroused both amusement and admiration. To some people he seemed to be holy, sacred—a Komsomol leader in torn sandals, in a calico shirt with an open collar, without a cap, in a torn leather coat, in a Budyenny-peaked Soviet soldier's helmet on which the red star was faded, pallid, as if from loss of blood. And he was tattered, unshaven, going about in wintertime in a raincoat with buttons hanging, he, Minister of Justice of the whole Ukraine, emerging from his car to enter his ministerial office.

He seemed helpless, to be not of this world, but people could remember how he had been listened to in prayerful awe during stormy meetings at the front, and how soldiers had followed him into the fire of Wrangel's machine guns.

He was a preacher, an apostle, and a warrior of the world-wide socialist revolution. For the sake of the Revolution, he, without quavering, was prepared to give up his life, a woman's love, all those closest to him. There was only one thing he could not give up—happiness: he would have been happy to sacrifice everything on earth a human being holds dear for the sake of the Revolution, to march for its sake straight into a bonfire.

The imminent new world order seemed infinitely beautiful to him, and for its sake Mekler was ready to undertake the most pitiless violence.

He himself, in the essence of his being, was a kind, good-natured person. He would not even crush a mosquito that sucked his blood, but would drive it off with a delicate snap of his fingers. If he caught a bedbug at the scene of its crime, he would wrap it in a piece of paper and throw it away outside.

He served the good and the Revolution in blood, and without mercy.

Because of his revolutionary principles, he imprisoned his father and testified against him before the collegium of the provincial Cheka. He turned his back cruelly and implacably on his sister when she begged him to help her husband, who had been arrested as a saboteur.

In his meekness he was merciless to those who had different ideas and concepts. In his eyes the Revolution was helpless, childishly trusting, surrounded by treachery, the cruelty of villains, the dirt of corrupters.

He was merciless to the enemies of the Revolution.

There was only one stain on his revolutionary conscience: Keeping it secret from the Party, he had helped his old mother, the widow of that father whom the police had shot, and when she died, he had paid for a religious funeral. This had been her last, pitiful request.

His vocabulary, the shape of his ideas, his actions, all were born out of books written for the revolutionary cause, out of revolutionary law, revolutionary morality, the poetry of the Revolution and its strategy, the forward advance of its soldiers, its insights, its songs.

Through the eyes of the Revolution he looked upon the starry heavens and on April bursting into leaf in the birch trees; from that most sweet cup he drank the loveliness of first love; and in the light of its wisdom, he saw and recognized the battle of the patricians and the slaves, of the feudal lords and the serfs, the class struggle of the factory owners and the proletarians. The Revolution was his mother, tenderly beloved of him, and it was his sun, his fate.

And so the Revolution put him in a cell in the Internal Prison—the Lubyanka—and knocked out eight of his teeth, trampled him with jackboots, cursed him with the foulest of Russian obscenities. Calling him a mangy cur, it demanded that he, its son, its loving apostle, confess to being a secret poisoner of the Revolution, its deadly enemy.

Of course, he did not renounce the Revolution. He did not tremble even for one moment during interrogations lasting a hundred hours, and he did not shudder when he lay on the floor of the interrogation chamber and saw, next to his nose and his bloodied mouth, the cleaned, polished, chrome-leather toe of the officer's jackboot.

The Revolution was crude, stupid, and cruel in those interrogations under torture that went on for days at a time, and the loyalty and meek submissiveness to the Revolution on the part of the Bolshevik Lev Mekler aroused its rage.

In the same way, a man whose mongrel dog keeps following him flies into a rage and tries to drive her away. First he speeds up his stride; then he shouts at the dog and stamps his feet; then he shakes his fist and throws stones at her. The dog retreats and stops, and when, after another hundred steps or so, the master looks behind him, he sees that the crippled dog has kept right on limping after him, wagging her tail.

And to her master the most repulsive and hateful thing about her love is the look in her dog's eyes: meek, sad, loving, fanatically loyal.

That love arouses the master's rage! The dog sees his rage and cannot understand it. She is incapable of grasping that, having committed an unimaginable injustice, he wants to let his conscience relax at least a little. This meekness, this submissiveness and loyalty, have driven him to the point of insanity. Because of her love the master hates the dog more than he hated the very wolves against which she defended the home of his youth. And out of cruelty, he wants to choke off her love.

But the dog keeps on following him, shocked by his sudden, inexplicable cruelty.

Why?

And the dog is quite unable to comprehend that the sudden hate directed against her is not meaningless but is altogether rational.

A law is manifested in this hate—clear, mathematical logic. Only to the dog does it seem a delusion, a spell. She even feels badly on her master's account and wants to help him get over his bad mood. She is quite incapable of going away from him. After all, she loves her master.

And by this time the master has realized that the dog will not let him alone and that the only thing left to do is to choke her, shoot her.

And in order that the execution of this adoring dog should not hurt his conscience or arouse the condemnation of his neighbors, the master decides to turn the dog into his enemy by artificial means. Let this dog, before she dies, confess that she wanted to bite him, her master.

It is much easier to kill an enemy than a friend.

After all, in that first house of his, which he had built in the midst of grim, somber, abandoned ruins, in the home of his youth, in the home of his pure prayers, this dog had been his friend, his guard, his inseparable companion.

So let this dog confess that she was plotting with the wolves.

And in her last death cries, as she is being choked to death with a rope, she looks upon her master with meekness, gentleness, and love, with a faith equal to that which led the first Christian martyrs to their deaths.

And even then she never understands the simple truth. The master had left the home of his youthful enthusiasm and prayer, and had moved into a house of granite and glass, and his village mongrel had become an absurdity for him, she had become a burden, and even more than a burden. She had become a danger. So he killed her.

20

The years passed, and the fog lifted, and what had been accomplished could be seen clearly. What had looked like chaos, insanity, self-destruction, the concatenation of unfortunate circumstances, the events whose mysterious, tragic meaninglessness had driven people mad, became recognizable step by step as the clear, precise, obvious attributes of the new life.

The fate of the generation of the Revolution was revealed in a new light, logically, without mysticism. Only now did Ivan Grigoryevich begin to grasp that new national destiny which had risen from the bones of the annihilated generation.

That Bolshevik generation of the Civil War period had been formed in the days of the Revolution; where the concept of the "World Commune" held absolute sway; in the midst of the hungry and inspired *subbotniki.* It took unto itself the heritage of World War and Civil War—destruction, famine, typhus, anarchy, rampant crime. Through

Lenin's lips it proclaimed the existence of a Party that could set Russia on a new path. Without hesitation it accepted as its inheritance centuries of Russian tyranny, throughout which generations had been born and had died knowing one right only—"serf right," the right of the master over the serf.

Under Lenin's leadership that Bolshevik generation had taken part in the dissolution of the Constituent Assembly and the destruction of those democratic revolutionary parties which had struggled against Russian absolutism.

That Bolshevik generation of the Civil War did not believe in freedom of the individual, freedom of speech, freedom of the press—not in the context of bourgeois Russia. Like Lenin, it regarded as nonsense, as nothing, those freedoms of which many revolutionary workers and intellectuals had dreamed.

The young state crushed the democratic parties, clearing the path for Soviet construction. And by the end of the twenties, those parties were completely liquidated, and the people imprisoned under the Czar had been returned to prison and sent off to hard labor. And then, in 1930, the ax of the total collectivization of agriculture fell. And soon the ax fell again, this time on the Bolshevik generation of the Civil War. Only a small fraction of it survived—and its soul, at any rate its faith in the "World Commune," its revolutionary, romantic strength, departed with those who perished in 1937. The ones who survived made their adjustment to the new times, to the new people.

And the new people did not believe in the Revolution. They were not children of the Revolution. They were the children of the state the Revolution had created.

The new state did not require holy apostles, fanatic, inspired builders, faithful, devout disciples. The new state did not even require servants—just clerks. One of the state's concerns, in fact, was that its clerks so often turned out to be very petty indeed, and cheating, thieving types to boot.

Terror and dictatorship swallowed up those who had created them. And the state, intended as the means to an end, itself turned out to be the end. The people who created it had conceived of it as a means to the realization of their ideals. But it turned out that their dreams, their ideals, were merely a means, a tool, of the great and dread state. Instead of being a servant, as it was meant to be, the state had become a grim tyrant.

The people weren't the ones who needed the terror of 1919, who destroyed freedom of speech and of the press, who required the death of millions of peasants—for the peasants made up the largest segment of the people. It was not the people who in 1937 needed prisons and camps crammed to overflowing, who needed the ruinous resettlement in the taiga of the Crimean Tatars, the Kalmyks, the Balkars, the Russified Bulgarians and Greeks, the Chechens, and the Volga Germans. Nor were the people the ones who destroyed the freedom to plant and sow as one pleased and the workers' right to strike. Nor was it the people who heaped up all those monstrous taxes and surtaxes and levies on the production cost of consumer goods.

The state had become the master. What had been envisioned as national in form had become national in content; it had become the essence. And the socialist element, which had been envisaged as the content, had been forced out, reduced to mere phraseology, mere external form, a shell. And it was with tragic clarity that the sacred law of all life defined itself: freedom of the individual human being is higher than anything else, and there is no goal, no purpose in the world, for which it may be sacrificed.

21

It was strange. When Ivan Grigoryevich thought about 1937, or about the women who were sentenced to hard labor on their husbands' account, or about total collectivization and the famine in the countryside, or about the laws that imposed prison sentences on workers who were twenty minutes late to work, or condemned peasants to eight years in camp for taking a few stalks of grain, he did not see in his mind's eye the mustached man in jackboots and field shirt—Stalin.

He saw Lenin, and it was as though Lenin had not for one moment died on January 21, 1924.

Sometimes Ivan Grigoryevich jotted down his thoughts about Lenin and Stalin in a school notebook left behind by Alyesha.

All the triumphs of Party and state were bound up with the name of Lenin. But all the cruelty inflicted on the nation also lay—tragically—on Lenin's shoulders.

His revolutionary passion, his speeches, his writings, his slogans, affirmed and justified the events in the countryside, and 1937, and the new bureaucracy, and the new petite bourgeoisie, and the slave labor of prisoners.

And gradually, over the years, and against his will, Lenin's features changed; the countenance of the student Volodya Ulyanov, of the young Marxist Tulin, of the Siberian exile, of the revolutionary émigré, of the publicist and thinker, Vladimir Ilich Lenin, the countenance of the man who proclaimed the era of the world-wide socialist revolution, the creator of the revolutionary dictatorship in Russia which liquidated all the revolutionary parties except the one he considered the most revolutionary of all, who liquidated the Constituent Assembly which represented all classes and parties of postrevolutionary Russia, and created the Soviets in which, according to his concept, only revolutionary workers and peasants would be represented—gradually, over the years, the countenance of the man who had done all that changed.

The Leninist traits, familiar from the portraits of him, changed too.

Lenin's cause continued, and, as it did, the face of the dead Lenin involuntarily acquired the traits being acquired by the cause he had launched.

He was an intellectual. He had come from a family of the working intelligentsia. His sisters, his brothers were members of the working revolutionary intelligentsia. His elder brother, Alexander, of the narodnaya volya, had become a hero and sacred martyr of the Revolution.

The writers of memoirs report that as the leader of the Revolution, the creator of the Party, the head of the Soviet government, he was still unchangingly modest and simple in his ways. He did not smoke and he did not drink, and in all likelihood he had never in his life given vent to unprintable profanity. His leisure, his diversions, were pure, like those of a university student—music, the theater, books, walks. His clothes were invariably democratic, almost the clothes of a poor man.

Could it have been he who used to climb to the upper tiers of the theater, wearing a wrinkled necktie and an old jacket; who listened to the "Appassionata"; who read and reread *War and Peace;* who was so dear to his mother's heart and was the Volodya beloved by his sisters—was it really he who went on to found the state which adorned with the Order of Lenin, its highest decoration, the chests of Yagoda, Yezhov, Beriya, Merkulov, and Abakumov? Do not forget that in 1953 the Order of Lenin was awarded to Lidiya Timashuk on the very anniversary of the death of Vladimir Ilich: did that symbolize the withering, the exhaustion, of Lenin's cause, or its triumph?

The years of the Five-Year Plans passed, decades passed, and enormous events, crammed with white-hot, steaming relevance and contemporaneity, congealed and hardened in whole blocks and boulders, encased in the cement of time, and were transformed into the history of the Soviet state:

> Lenin's portraits are not to be seen.
> They weren't there, nor are they yet;
> The ages, it seems, will have to fill in
> The unfinished portrait.

Did the poet understand the tragic meaning of his lines about Lenin? Those attributes so remarked on by his biographers and by those who mentioned him in their memoirs, those traits which seemed so very basic, charming millions of hearts and minds, turned out to be quite incidental to the course of history. The history of the Russian state did not choose for its purposes Lenin's endearing, humane and human qualities, but cast them aside as unwanted trash. The history of the state had no use for Lenin's rapt listening to the "Appassionata," nor his love of *War and Peace,* nor his democratic modesty, nor his sincere attentiveness to the little people around him—secretaries, chauffeurs—nor his chats with peasant children, nor his kindness to pets, nor his heartfelt pain when Martov was transformed from friend into enemy.

And everything about him that had been regarded as temporary, and accidental, and present only because of the special circumstances of the underground and the harsh struggle of the first Soviet years, turned out to be permanent, decisive, basic.

Just such a trait, never mentioned by the writers of memoirs, resulted, for example, in his ordering a search of the dying Plekhanov's quarters. Such traits determined his absolute intolerance of political democracy; these were the traits which became dominant.

A factory owner or a merchant who has moved up from the peasantry, who lives in his private mansion and sails on his private yacht, still retains some traces of his peasant origin—his love of sour cabbage soup, of kvass, of crudely vivid folk phrases. A marshal in a gold-embroidered uniform still likes makhorka and the simple humor of soldiers' swearing.

But do these preferences significantly affect the fate of factories and the people who work in them? Do they significantly influence the movement of stock prices or the movement of armies?

Not through love of sour cabbage soup or makhorka is

the wealth of industrialists or the glory of generals won.

One author of a memoir of Lenin describes going on a Sunday walk in the Swiss mountains with Vladimir Ilich. Panting from the steepness of the climb, they reached a summit and sat down on a rock. It seemed as though Vladimir Ilich's gaze was taking in each small detail of the Alpine beauty. The young woman assumed raptly that poetry was flooding Vladimir Ilich's soul. And suddenly he sighed, and said: "How those Mensheviks are pouring filth on us!"

This tender episode says something about Lenin's character and nature: on one side of the scales was God's good world, and on the other—the Party.

October selected those traits of Vladimir Ilich that it required, and October cast out those it did not need.

Throughout the whole history of the Russian revolutionary movement, such qualities as love of the people, inherent in many of the revolutionary intellectuals, whose meekness and readiness to endure suffering seemed unequaled since the epoch of the first Christians, mingled with diametrically opposite attributes, and these, too, were inherent in many Russian revolutionaries—contempt for and disregard of human suffering, subservience to abstract theories, the determination to annihilate not merely enemies but those comrades who deviated even slightly from complete acceptance of the particular abstraction in question. Sectarian determinism, the readiness to suppress today's living freedom for the sake of an imaginary freedom tomorrow and to violate universal canons of morality for the sake of the world to be—all these aspects were evident in the character of Pestel, Bakunin, Nechayev, and in some of the statements and actions of the narodnaya volya disciples.

No, it was not love alone, not compassion alone, that led

these people on the path of the Revolution, and the sources of their personalities lie deep within the thousand-year depths of Russia.

Such characters existed in former times too, but it was the twentieth century which brought them from the wings onto the main stage of life.

This sort of person behaves among other people as a surgeon does in the wards of a hospital. His interest in the patients, their fathers, wives, mothers, his jokes, his conversations, his taking part in fund-raising drives on behalf of homeless children or retired workers living on their pensions—any and all of this is meaningless and superficial, a mask. His soul is really in his knife.

And the essence of these people lies in their fanatical faith in the surgeon's knife. The surgeon's knife—that is the great theoretician, the archphilosopher of the twentieth century.

During his fifty-four years, Lenin not only listened to the "Appassionata" sonata, reread *War and Peace,* engaged in heart-to-heart talks with peasant pilgrims, worried whether his secretary had a winter coat, and admired the Russian landscape. Yes, yes, of course—in addition to the image there is the real person.

And one can imagine a whole multitude of traits and peculiarities that Lenin revealed in his daily life, that life all people inevitably live, be they leaders of the people, specialists in stomatology, or cutters in factories manufacturing women's coats.

These traits are in evidence at various times of day, when a person washes his face in the morning, when he eats his hot cereal, when he looks out the window at a pretty woman whose skirts have been caught by the wind, when he picks his teeth with a match, or reveals his jealousy of his wife and arouses her jealousy of him, when he examines his naked legs and feet in the bathtub and scratches his armpits, when he reads scraps of newspaper in the toilet and attempts to piece together the torn fragments, when he breaks wind and then coughs or sings in an effort to cover it up.

Such things happen in the lives of great people and insignificant people, and, obviously, they occurred in Lenin's life as well.

Perhaps Lenin's paunch was the result of eating a lot of macaroni and oil, preferring it to green vegetables.

Perhaps, quite unknown to the world, he had arguments with Nadezhda Konstantinovna Krupskaya, his wife, about washing his feet, cleaning his teeth, and changing a dirty shirt.

And it might perhaps be possible to break through all the walls erected around him, to get past the supposedly human, but in fact totally unreal, exalted image of the leader, and win through to the simple, plain, unvarnished, authentic essence of Lenin, that essence none of the memoirs has ever revealed.

But what would we gain from the knowledge, the discovery, of the genuine, everyday characteristics and peculiarities of Lenin's behavior in bathroom, dining room, bedroom? Would this knowledge help us acquire a more profound understanding of the leader of the new Russia, the founder of a new world order? Would knowing Lenin's character show us a real connection with the character of the state he founded? For that to be the case, we would have to assume that Lenin's traits as a political leader had equivalents in Lenin's traits as a private person. But such an assumption would be utterly arbitrary. And it cannot be made. After all, such a connection, if it exists at all, might just as well exist in a negative sense as in a positive one. It could as easily be an inverse relationship as a direct one.

So let us say that in his personal and private relations, when he spent the night with friends, when he gave a comrade help, Lenin invariably showed sensitivity, delicacy, gentleness, courtesy. And at the same time he consistently displayed rancor, pitilessness, and rudeness toward his political opponents. He never admitted the slightest possibility that his opponents were even slightly right about anything, or the least possibility of his being the least bit in the wrong.

"Mercenary . . . lackey . . . groveler . . . hireling . . . agent . . . Judas . . . bought for thirty pieces of silver."

These are some of the words Lenin would use about his opponents.

In an argument Lenin did not try to convince his opponents. In a quarrel or a dispute he did not even address his opponent. He addressed those who were witnessing the quarrel, and his purpose was to ridicule and compromise his opponent in their eyes. These witnesses might be a few of his intimates or thousands of delegates at a congress or millions of newspaper readers.

In a dispute Lenin was not trying to arrive at the truth. He wanted to win! He had a compulsion to win at any cost, and he was not choosy about the means. In order to win it was perfectly all right to trip someone up from behind, or, symbolically, slap his face, or beat him over the head.

And it turned out that Lenin's everyday, ordinary, domestic traits were utterly unconnected with his traits as leader of a new world order.

Consequently, when the difference of opinion spread

from the pages of the magazines and newspapers to the streets, to the grain fields, to the battlefields, there, too, all tactics, no matter how cruel and harsh, were legitimate.

Lenin's intolerance, Lenin's implacable drive to achieve his purpose, his contempt for freedom, his cruelty toward those who held different opinions, and his capacity to wipe off the face of the earth, without trembling, not only fortresses, but entire counties, districts, and provinces that questioned his orthodox truth—all these were characteristics of Volodya Ulyanov Lenin. And they had deep roots.

All his talents, all his will and his passion, were directed to one purpose—to seize power.

To this end he sacrificed everything. And to this end—to seize power—he offered as a sacrifice, he killed, what was most sacred in Russia: Russia's freedom. And how could Russia's freedom, eight-month-old infant that it was, born with the heritage of a thousand years of slavery, have the experience to cope with all that?

The traits of the intellectual, which had seemed to be the genuine content of the Leninist soul and the Leninist personality, turned out to be external and insignificant form; they vanished just as soon as things got down to real business, and his true character was made manifest in his unbending, unyielding, iron, frenzied will.

What led Lenin on the path of Revolution? Was it love of people? The desire to fight against the poverty of the peasantry, the poverty and servitude of the workers? Was it faith in the truth of Marxism, faith in the truth of his Party?

To him, the Russian Revolution did not mean freedom for Russia. And yet that power he strove so passionately to achieve was not something he craved for his private use.

And this fact reveals one of his particular characteristics: complexity of character deriving from simplicity of character.

To thirst for power with such might and main, a man has to have enormous political vanity and an enormous love of power. These attributes are crude and simple. But Lenin, in whom the thirst for power burned, and who was capable of everything and anything in his struggle to seize it, was extremely modest personally, and he did not seek for himself the power he won. Which is where the simplicity ends and the complexity begins.

If we imagine Lenin the private individual as identical with Lenin the politician, we are confronted by a primitive, crude personality—impudent, highhanded, power-loving, pitiless, madly ambitious, dogmatically shrill.

And if we were to expect these traits to show up in everyday relationships with wife, mother, friends, neighbors, and others, it would be horrible to imagine.

But things were quite different. The man in the arena of world affairs turned out to be the exact opposite of the man in his personal life. Plus and minus, minus and plus.

Yes, things were quite different, and, in many ways, tragic.

Mad political ambition, combined with an old jacket, with a glass of watery tea, with a university student's garret.

The capacity to trample an opponent in the mud with no hesitation, to put down an opponent in an argument, are paradoxically combined with a kind smile and shy sensitivity.

Implacable cruelty, contempt for the holy of holies of the Russian Revolution—freedom—and, in the breast of the very same man, a pure, youthful joy in beautiful music or a fine book.

There are three versions of Lenin. . . .

The first is the familiar deified image.

The second is the version created by his enemies: the monolithic simpleton, combining the cruel characteristics of the leader of a new world order with equally primitive, crude traits in his everyday life. These were the only traits his enemies could see in him.

And last is the third Lenin, who seems to me the closest to actual reality—and this Lenin is not by any means easy to comprehend.

22

To understand Lenin it is first necessary to relate his character to the myth of the Russian national character, and then to the fate, the character, of Russian history.

In his asceticism and natural modesty Lenin was akin to the Russian "wanderers"—the wandering religious pilgrims of time immemorial. In his straightforwardness, directness, and faith he was akin to the folk ideal of a great religious teacher. In his attachment to Russian nature, to its forests and meadows, he was akin to the Russian peasantry. His receptivity to the world of Western thought, to Hegel and Marx, his capacity to absorb and to express the spirit of the West, was a deeply Russian trait proclaimed by Chaadayev, the very same universal receptivity Dostoyevsky could see in Pushkin. That receptivity makes him akin to Pushkin. And it was also a characteristic of Peter the Great.

In his susceptibility to being possessed and obsessed, in his intensity of conviction, Lenin was akin to the frenzy of Avvakum, to Avvakum's faith. And Avvakum was a native-born Russian phenomenon.

In the last century Russian thinkers looked for an explanation of Russia's historical path in the special traits of the Russian national character, in the Russian soul, in Russian religious fervor.

Chaadayev, one of the wisest men of the nineteenth century, hailed the ascetic, sacrificial spirit of Russian Christianity, its Byzantine character, unmuddied and undiluted by borrowed elements.

Dostoyevsky believed the quality of being universally human and striving for the universality of all humanity was the real basis of the Russian soul.

The Russian twentieth century loves to repeat the prophecies about Russia uttered by nineteenth-century Russian thinkers and prophets—Gogol, Chaadayev, Belinsky, Dostoyevsky.

Yes. And who, for that matter, would not enjoy repeating such things about himself?

The prophets of the nineteenth century predicted that Russia would lead the spiritual development not only of Europe but of the entire world.

These prophets were not referring to Russian military glory, but to the glory of the Russian heart, to Russian faith, the Russian example:

> The flying troika.
>
> It is for the Russian soul, universally human and all-uniting, to make room within itself, in brotherly love, for all our brothers, and, perhaps, in the end, to speak the last word in our great common harmony, the final agreement in brotherhood of all tribes under the laws of the gospel of Christ!
>
> . . . When we come to take our natural place among the peoples chosen to act among mankind, not only by virtue of our tyrants, but by virtue of our ideas!

> Russia, are you not hurtling along like a spirited troika outrunning all pursuit? Beneath you the road smokes, and bridges thunder. . . .

And right at this point, Chaadayev, in a stroke of genius, drew attention to the astounding fact of Russian history: "the colossal fact of the step-by-step, gradual enserfment of our peasantry, which represented the strictly logical consequence of our history."

Implacable suppression of the individual ran continuously throughout Russia's thousand-year history. Slave subjugation of the individual to the state and to the sovereign. Yes, and these traits, too, were seen and recognized by the Russian prophets.

And along with the suppression of the human being by the prince, by the estate and serf owner, by the sovereign and the state, the Russian prophets professed to find a purity, profundity, clarity unknown in the Western world, the strength of Christ in the Russian soul. The prophets prophesied a great and bright future for that Russian soul. They agreed that the Christian ideal had been embodied in the Russian soul in a stateless, ascetic, Byzantine, non-Western form, and that the forces inherent in the Russian soul would express themselves as a powerful influence on the peoples of Europe, that they would purify, transform, and enlighten, in the spirit of brotherhood, the life of the Western world, which would follow trustingly and joyfully the path the Russian soul had pointed to. These prophecies of the best minds and hearts of Russia had one fatal fallacy in common. All saw the strength of the Russian soul, and prophesied its significance for the world, and all failed to see that the particular qualities of the Russian soul did not derive from freedom, and that the Russian soul had been a slave for a thousand years. What could the slave of a thousand years give the world, even a slave become omnipotent?

And the nineteenth century, it seemed, had brought closer the time foretold by the Russian prophets when Russia, so accessible, so open, so eagerly absorbing alien spiritual influences, was preparing to influence the world.

For one hundred years Russia absorbed the borrowed idea of freedom. For one hundred years Russia drank down, through Pestel, Rylyeyev, Herzen, Chernyshevsky, Lavrov, Bakunin, through her writers, through the martyred Zhelyabov, Sofia Perovskaya, Timofei Mikhailov, N. I. Kibalchich, through Lenin, Martov, and Chernov, through her intellectuals, university students, progressive workers —through them all, Russia drank down the idea of freedom evolved by Western philosophers. This concept was spread by books, and by university faculties, and by university students in Paris and Heidelberg, and it was spread by the boots of Bonaparte's soldiers, by engineers and enlightened merchants, and by impoverished Westerners employed in Russia as teachers, tutors, governesses, whose conviction of their own human dignity aroused the envious astonishment of Russian princes.

And so, fertilized by the ideas of freedom and of the individual's human dignity, the Russian Revolution came into being.

And what did the Russian soul make of the Western world's ideas, how did it transform them within itself, in what form did it crystallize them, what shoot was ready to sprout from the subconscious of history?

"Russia, whither are you flying? . . . But there is no answer."

Like prospective brides being shown off to their suitors, there paraded before the young Russia, which had cast off the chains of czarism, dozens, hundreds, of revolutionary teachings, faiths, party leaders, prophecies, programs. . . . And the leaders of Russian progress looked passionately and entreatingly into the faces of the brides parading past them. They stood in a wide circle, all kinds—moderates, fanatics, trudoviks, narodniks, the champions of the industrial workers, the protectors of the peasantry, enlightened factory owners, enlightened churchmen, mad anarchists.

Invisible threads bound them, although they sometimes did not sense this themselves, to the ideas of the Western constitutional monarchies, parliaments, educated cardinals and bishops, factory owners, learned agriculturalists, trade-union leaders, preachers, and university professors.

And the great slave fixed his seeking, doubting, evaluating gaze on Lenin. And Lenin became the chosen one.

He was the one who had guessed, as in a fairy tale, Russia's puzzling dream, Russia's concept and design.

Lenin became Russia's chosen one because he chose Russia and because Russia chose him.

Russia followed him because he promised her mountains of gold and rivers flowing with wine; she followed him willingly at first, believing in him, along his gay, intoxicating path, lit by the burning mansions of estate owners, only later holding back a bit, more reluctantly, looking backward, becoming ever more fearful of the path opening before her, but feeling more and more strongly the iron hand that led her.

And so he marched forward, imbued with his apostolic faith, leading Russia in his wake without grasping the strange contradiction he had fallen into. In Russia's submissiveness in following him, in Russia's new obedience in the aftermath of the Czar's overthrow, in her Russian pliancy which could drive one out of one's mind, everything he had brought to Russia from the freedom-loving, revolutionary West drowned, perished, was transformed.

It seemed to him that his unshakable dictatorial power guaranteed the purity and the preservation of what he believed in, of what he had brought his country.

He rejoiced in this power and he equated it with the rightness of his faith, and then suddenly, in a fleeting moment, he saw with horror that in his unchallengeable power, as it interacted with the soft Russian subservience and suggestibility, his own impotence lay.

And the harsher his onward stride, the heavier his hand, and the more Russia submitted to his studied revolutionary violence, the more rapidly waned his actual power to struggle against the truly satanic force of Russia's serf past.

Like a thousand-year-old spirituous liquor waxing stronger as it ages, the slave foundation within the Russian soul waxed even stronger. Like aqua regia, its yellow fumes dissolving gold, it dissolved the metal and the salts of human dignity and transformed the inner life of the individual Russian.

For nine hundred years the broad and open expanses of the Russian land created, in the superficial view, an impression of breadth of soul, daring, freedom. They were, in fact, only the mute retort of slavery.

For nine hundred years Russia kept migrating from its remote forest settlements, its soot-laden, chimneyless "black" huts, its backwoods log mansions, to the Urals' metallurgical works, to Donbass coal mines, to St. Petersburg palaces, to the Hermitage, to frigates, to steam boilers.

Superficially, the impression was of growing enlightenment and increasing rapprochement with the West.

But the more Russian life came to resemble, superficially, that of the West, and the more the roar of Russian factories, the click of the wheels of tarantasses and trains, the flapping of ships' sails, the gleam of Russian palace windows took on the aspect of life in the West, the greater grew the unseen chasm between the essence of Russian life and that of Europe.

This chasm lay in the fact that Western development was based on a growth in freedom, while Russia's was based on the intensification of slavery.

The history of humanity is the history of human freedom. The growth in human might is expressed, first and foremost, in the growth of human freedom. Freedom is not, as Engels thought, "the recognition of necessity." Freedom is the opposite of necessity. Freedom is necessity overcome. Progress is, in essence, the progress of human freedom. Yes, and after all, life itself is freedom. The evolution of life is the evolution of freedom.

Russia's development displayed a peculiar trait—it became the development of nonfreedom. Year by year serfdom became harsher and more cruel for the peasantry; the peasant's claim to the land lessened steadily, and all the while Russian science, technology, and learning kept advancing in step with the growth of Russian slavery.

The birth of Russian statehood was marked by the final enslavement—enserfment—of the peasants: the last landmark of freedom of the peasants was abolished, November 26, Yuryev Day, representing an annual two-week period when the peasant was legally free to leave his landlord or master and thereby opt out of serfdom.

The number of "free" or "wandering" people not yet enserfed kept dwindling, and the number of slaves kept increasing—and all the while Russia began to move out onto the broad path of European history. The person bound at first to the land soon became bound to the landowner and then to the person in the sovereign's official bureaucracy who represented the state and the army; and the master was given the legal right to pass judgment on his serfs, and, later, the right to sentence them to the Moscow torture (so-called even four full centuries ago), which consisted in hanging a man up with his arms tied behind his back and beating him with the knout. And Russian metallurgy waxed, and grain depots grew larger, and the state and its armies increased in might, and the dawn of Russian military glory arrived and literacy spread.

The mighty work of Peter, who built the foundations of Russian scientific and military progress, involved an equal increase in the severity of serfdom. Peter reduced the peasant serfs who worked the land to the even lower level of the household slaves—the landless house servants of the estate owners. He made serfs of the "wandering people." He put an end to the independence of the remaining independent peasant-farmers, both North and South. Not only did the oppression of the serfs owned by landed noblemen grow heavier; the bondage of the large numbers of serfs owned by the state was also made more burdensome; and all this helped to provide funds for Peter's program of education and progress. Peter thought he was bringing the West and

Russia closer, and he was. But the abyss between freedom and nonfreedom kept growing wider.

Then came the brilliant age of Catherine, epoch of the flowering of Russian arts and Russian enlightenment, the age in which serfdom reached its highest level of development.

And so it was that in a thousand-year-long chain Russian slavery and Russian progress were shackled to each other. Every move forward to reach the light only deepened the black pit of serfdom.

The nineteenth century, however, was a very special epoch in Russia's life.

That century shook the basic principle of Russian life—the tie between progress and serfdom.

Russian revolutionary thinkers greatly underestimated the importance of the nineteenth century's emancipation of the serfs. That act, as the following century showed, was more genuinely revolutionary than the October Revolution. Emancipation shook the millennial foundations of Russian life, as neither Peter nor Lenin could shake them.

After the emancipation of the serfs, the revolutionary leaders, the intelligentsia, the university students, plunged into the struggle for a human dignity unknown in Russia, for progress without slavery. But this new development was wholly alien to the Russian past, and no one knew what kind of Russia would arise were it to reject the thousand-year-old link of progress and slavery.

In February, 1917, the path of freedom lay straight ahead for Russia. And Russia chose Lenin.

The shattering of Russian life carried out by Lenin was thoroughgoing. Lenin destroyed the way of life dominated by the outlook of the landed nobles; he destroyed the factory owners and merchants.

Yet Lenin himself was the slave of Russian history, and he preserved that link between progress and slavery which has historically been Russia's curse.

The only true revolutionaries are those who seek to destroy this keystone of the old Russia.

So it was that his revolutionary obsession, his fanatical Marxist faith, his total intolerance of those who thought differently, led Lenin to further the colossal development of that very Russia which he hated with all the strength of his fanatical soul.

How tragic that a man who so loved Tolstoi and Beethoven should take part in a new enslavement of the peasants and workers, and in reducing to the status of lackeys outstanding men of culture—such as Alexei Tolstoi, the chemist Semyenov, the composer Shostakovich.

Thus the debate begun by the apostles of Russian freedom was decided once again, and Russian slavery once again proved invincible.

Lenin's victory became his defeat.

But Lenin's was more than a Russian tragedy—it was a world tragedy.

Could Lenin have guessed in the hour of the Revolution he set in motion that it might not be Russia that followed in the footsteps of a socialist Europe, but that clandestine Russian slavery would itself spread outside Russia and become the torch to light new paths for all mankind?

Russia no longer drank in the free spirit of the West. Instead, the West watched, hypnotized, the spectacle of Russian progress proceeding along the path of nonfreedom.

The world saw the fascinating simplicity of this path. The world saw the strength of this people's state built upon nonfreedom.

And it might have seemed as though the predictions of the nineteenth-century Russian prophets had indeed come true. But how strangely, how terribly, it had all turned out!

The Leninist synthesis of non-freedom and socialism shook the world more violently than the release of atomic energy.

The European preachers of nationalist revolutions saw and understood the flame in the East. First the Italians, and then the Germans, proceeded to develop the concept of national socialism in their own ways.

And the flame kept spreading—to Asia, to Africa. It turned out that nations and states can develop in the cause of power and in defiance of freedom.

This, of course, was not food for the healthy. It was a narcotic for failures, for the sick, weak, backward, downtrodden.

The thousand-year Russian law of development thereby became, by the will and passion of Lenin, a world-wide law.

Such was the evil fate of history.

Lenin's intolerance, forcefulness, firmness in opposition to those who differed from him, his contempt for freedom, the fanaticism of his faith, his mercilessness to his enemies—everything that brought victory to his cause—had been forged in the thousand-year depths of Russian serfdom, Russian nonfreedom. And alongside those far-reaching factors of his personality coexisted the traits of a dear, modest, Russian working intellectual, traits which had charmed so many millions, and were insubstantial, signifying nothing.

And what does it mean? Is the Russian soul still a riddle? No!

Was there ever any riddle? What kind of riddle can the soul formed in slavery really be?

Is this exclusively a Russian law? Was it only in Russia that national progress was based on the intensification of slavery? Of course not.

The law was determined by dozens and even hundreds of parameters circumscribing Russian history.

Had it happened that instead of Russians, say, Frenchmen, Germans, or Englishmen had been confined within those parameters, such as the forest and the steppe, the swamp and the plains, the field of magnetic attraction between Europe and Asia, and the tragic vastness of Russia, and had it been they, instead of the Russians, who had been compelled to move within these parameters for a thousand years, the law of their history would have become the same as Russia's. Nor have the Russians alone come to know this road. There are more than a few peoples in the world who, either distantly and vaguely or closely and clearly, have experienced through harsh fate the bitterness of the Russian path.

It is time for those who would understand Russia to understand that a thousand years of slavery have alone created the mystique of the Russian soul.

In the Russian fascination with Byzantine, ascetic purity, with Christian meekness, lives the unwitting admission of the permanence of Russian slavery. The sources of this Christian meekness and gentleness, of this Byzantine, ascetic purity, are the same as those of Leninist passion, fanaticism, and intolerance.

And that is why the nineteenth-century Russian prophets were so tragically mistaken. Where is it now, that "Russian soul," both "universally human and all-uniting," which, Dostoyevsky predicted, would "speak the last word in our great common harmony, the final agreement in brotherhood of all tribes under the laws of the gospel of Christ"?

Yes, and what was it anyway, good Lord, that universally human and all-uniting soul? Did the prophets of Russia ever imagine that their prophecies of the forthcoming holy triumph of the Russian soul would be realized, would actually materialize in the identical creaking of the barbed wire stretched around the Siberian taiga and around Auschwitz?

In so many ways, Lenin contradicted the great Russian prophets. He was infinitely far away from their concepts of meekness, Byzantine, Christian purity, and the laws of Christ's Gospel. But, surprisingly enough, he was at the same time at one with them. Traveling his separate path, he, too, made no effort to save Russia from its thousand-year bottomless quicksand of nonfreedom. Like them, he recognized the unalterability of Russian slavery.

The slave soul of the Russian lives in both Russian faith and Russian faithlessness, in the Russian's meek and gentle love for mankind and in Russian recklessness, hooliganism, and blind daring, in Russian miserliness and philistinism and in the Russian's patient capacity for hard work, in the Russian's ascetic purity and in the Russian talent for super-swindling and fraud, in the bravery of Russian warriors that is so awesome to the enemy and in the lack of human dignity in the Russian character, in the desperate revolt of Russian rebels and in the frenzy of Russian sectarians; the slave soul is present in the Leninist Revolution and in Lenin's passionate willingness to adopt the revolutionary teachings of the West, in Lenin's fanatic obsessions and in Leninist violence, and in the victories of the Leninist state.

Wherever slavery exists it gives birth to souls of the same kind.

What hope is there for Russia if even her greatest prophets cannot tell freedom from slavery?

What hope is there for Russia if her greatest geniuses see the bright and gentle beauty of her soul made manifest in her submissive acceptance of slavery?

What hope is there for Russia if Lenin, who transformed her most, did not destroy but strengthened the tie between Russian progress and Russian slavery?

When will Russia ever be free?

Perhaps never.

23

Lenin died, but Leninism did not. The power Lenin won did not pass from the hands of the Party. Lenin's comrades, aides, associates, and disciples continued the Leninist cause.

> Those he left behind
> had to bind with cement
> the land flooded by storm.
> In their case you'd not say Lenin had died.
> Death led them not to despair and grow weary.
> They went on doing Lenin's deeds,
> only more grimly than before.

Lenin left behind him the dictatorship of the Party he had established, the army, the militia-police force, the Cheka, the apparatus for eliminating illiteracy, the special schools for workers. He also left twenty-eight volumes of his works. And who, among his comrades-in-arms, would be best able to absorb and express the essence of Leninism? Who would take up and carry his banner?

Would it be the brilliant, stormy, magnificent Trotsky? Would it be the charming Bukharin, who was such a talented generalizer and theoretician? Would it be the practical practitioner of statesmanship, who was closest of all to the people's, the peasants' and the workers' interests, the ox-eyed Rykov? The expert of the workers' movement, the polemicist of international stature, Zinoviev?

The character, the spirit, of each of these men was close, was in harmony with one or another facet of Lenin's nature. But, as it turned out, those facets of his nature were not its determining essence, the heart of the new world being born.

In a fateful way it turned out that all those aspects of Lenin's character which were expressed in the personalities of Trotsky, Bukharin, Rykov, Zinoviev, and Kamenev proved to be seditious and led them all to the executioner's block.

The essence of Lenin's character did not lie in them. They shared Lenin's weakness, his eccentricity, illusions, but not the essence of the new order.

After all Lunacharsky shared Lenin's admiration for the "Appassionata" sonata and *War and Peace.* But it was not for poor Lunacharsky grimly to carry out the principal task of Lenin's Party. Historical fate did not pick out Trotsky, Bukharin, Rykov, Kamenev, or Zinoviev to express the Leninist quintessence.

Stalin's hatred for those leaders opposed to him was in reality hatred for those of Lenin's traits which contradicted his essence.

Stalin executed Lenin's closest friends and comrades-in-arms because each in his own way hindered the realization of Lenin's innermost essence.

In struggling with them, in executing them, it was as if he were struggling with Lenin and executing Lenin. But it was Stalin who victoriously affirmed and confirmed Lenin and Leninism, who raised the Leninist banner over Russia and secured it in place there.

24

The name of Stalin has been inscribed for all eternity in Russian history.

Postrevolutionary Russia, looking at Stalin, recognized itself.

Twenty-eight volumes of Lenin's works—speeches, reports, programs, economic and philosophical studies—were not nearly enough to enable Russia to discern herself and her fate. Chaos, beyond that of Babylon, was the outcome of combining Western revolution with the Russian law of development and progress.

Not only the Red sailors and Budyenny's cavalrymen, not only the Russian peasantry and workers, were helpless in trying to grasp the meaning of what was taking place. Lenin himself was no better off. The roar of the revolutionary storm, the laws of dialectical materialism, the logic of *Das Kapital*, merged and mingled with the blare of Russian accordions, the singing of popular revolutionary street songs, the hum of illegal samogon distilleries, and the appeals of lecturers and propagandists urging the sailors and students in the special workers' schools not to listen to the poisonous heresies of Kautsky, Cunov, and Hilferding.

Fire, rebellion, debauch, and violence, raging through Russia, churned up from the bottom of the Russian caldron the whole mass of spite and malice piled up through the centuries of Russia's serf suffering.

Out of the romance of the Revolution, out of the madness of the proletkult, out of the green samogon republics, out of all the intoxicated recklessness and the peasants' rebellion, out of the frenzy of the sailors on the *Almaz*, arose a new and powerful police chief such as Russia had never before known.

The passionate desire of the people to own the arable land, which Lenin had understood and fostered, was regarded with hostility by the state Lenin founded as being incompatible with itself. And the state dealt mercilessly and implacably with this striving of the people to own the land.

In 1930 the state Lenin founded became the indivisible owner of all lands, forests, and waters in the Soviet Union—and deprived the peasantry of the right to own any plowland.

Confusion, contradictions, and fog reigned not only at railway junctions, wharves, and on the roofs of the prisoner-transport trains, not only in the aspirations of the villagers and the excited minds of poets. There was just as much confusion in the area of revolutionary theory, in the striking contradictions between actual practice and the crystal-clear new theses of the Party's first theoretician.

The basic Leninist slogan was "All power to the Soviets!" But life itself revealed that the Soviets Lenin created had no power whatsoever—nor have they ever acquired any. They are a purely formal and auxiliary administrative apparatus.

The whole theoretical drive of the young Lenin was directed against the narodnaya volya, against the Social Revolutionaries, in an attempt to prove that Russia could not avoid the capitalist process of development. But in 1917 Lenin's whole drive was directed toward proving that Russia, bypassing the capitalist path with its concomitant democratic freedoms, must proceed along the path of the proletarian revolution.

Could Lenin have thought, as he founded the Comintern, and, at its Second Congress, proclaimed the slogan of world revolution, "Proletarians of the world, unite!," that he was preparing the ground for a titanic growth of national sovereignty beyond any ever before seen in world history?

This force of state nationalism and this mad nationalism on the part of masses of people deprived of freedom and human dignity became the principal lever, the thermonuclear warhead, of the new order, and determined the evil destiny of the twentieth century.

Stalin straightened out the minds of post-October, postrevolutionary Russia, and he handed out earrings to all the sisters. As for those who were not to be allowed earrings, he tore the earrings off along with their ears and their heads.

The Bolshevik Party was destined to become the Party of a national state. The merging of Party and state found its expression in Stalin's own identity. In Stalin, in his character, his personality, his mind, his will, the state expressed its own character, its own will, its own mind.

Seemingly, Stalin built the state Lenin had founded in his, Stalin's, own image. But this was not, of course, the heart of the matter—his image was actually the likeness of the state, and that is precisely why he became its master.

But sometimes, evidently, especially as he neared the end of his life, he felt that the state was his personal servant.

In Stalin, in the Asian despot and the European Marxist combined in his personality and character, the nature of the Soviet state system was expressed precisely and uniquely. The Russian national principle in Russian history was embodied in Lenin. And the principle of the Soviet Russian state system found its embodiment in Stalin. The Russian state system, born of Asia but arraying itself in Western clothing, is not an historic phenomenon. It is a suprahistorical phenomenon.

Its principle is universal, unchanging, applicable to all the different reincarnations of Russia during its thousand-year history. With Stalin's help such revolutionary categories as dictatorship, terror, the rejection of bourgeois liberties—all those things which Lenin had considered temporary, transitory expedients—were transformed into the permanent basis of Soviet life, became its essence, and were absorbed into Russia's historical, thousand-year continuum of nonfreedom.

With Stalin's help these categories became the content of the Russian state, and the Social Democratic vestiges were reduced to mere matters of form, a shell, a stage set.

All the pitiless traits of enslaved Russia, Stalin gathered unto himself.

In his unimaginable ferocity and cruelty, in his unbelievable falsity and treachery, in his talent for playing the hypocrite, in his cherished resentments and his vengefulness, in his crudeness, rudeness, humor—behold the Asiatic tyrant.

In his knowledge of revolutionary ideas and texts, in his use of the terminology of the progressive West, in his familiarity with the literature and the theater beloved by

Russia's democratic intelligentsia, in his quotations from Gogol and Shchedrin, in his mastery of the most delicate and complex conspiratorial tricks, in his amorality, he embodied a revolutionary of the Nechayev type, a person for whom any means at all were justified by the ends. But even Nechayev, of course, would have shuddered to see to what monstrous lengths Joseph Stalin developed the Nechayev principle.

In his faith in administrative documents and police power as the moving force in life, in his secret passion for uniforms and medals, in his unexampled contempt for human dignity, in his deification of a system based on a rigid and autocratic bureaucracy, in his readiness to kill a man on behalf of the holy letter of the law, and immediately thereafter to flout the law with monstrous and capricious violence—in all these respects he embodied the police boss, the gendarme spirit.

In the combination of these three Stalins, the Stalin personality lay.

And it was these three Stalins who created the system of the Stalinist state: a system in which the law is a weapon of tyranny only and in which tyranny is the law; a system whose roots go back a thousand years into Russia's serf past, whereby peasants were transformed into slaves, to the Tatar yoke which made slaves even of those who played the role of prince above the peasants; a system bordered on one side by faithless, treacherous, vengeful, hypocritical, and cruel Asia and on the other by enlightened, democratic, mercenary, and mercantile Europe.

This Asiatic in kid boots, quoting Shchedrin, living by the laws of tribal vengeance, and at the same time adept in the vocabulary of revolution, brought clarity into the post-

October chaos by realizing and expressing his own character through the character of the state. The underlying principle of the state he built was the absence of freedom.

In this state, not only the national minorities but the Russian people as well have no national freedom. Where there is no individual human freedom there can be no national freedom, since national freedom requires, to begin with, the freedom of each human being.

In this state there is no sense of community. Community is founded on free intimacy among people and free antagonism, and in a state without freedom, freedom of intimacy and of antagonism is unthinkable.

The thousand-year-old principle, in accordance with which Russian enlightenment, science, and industrial might increased by virtue of the increase in nonfreedom, the principle nourished in ancient boyar Russia, by Ivan the Terrible, by Peter, by Catherine, this principle attained its ultimate triumph under Stalin.

And it is truly astonishing that Stalin, who had so completely annihilated freedom, nonetheless continued to be afraid of it.

It may have been his fear of freedom that compelled Stalin to display his truly incredible hypocrisy.

Stalin's hypocrisy clearly conveyed the hypocrisy of his state. And this hypocrisy was expressed principally in the pretense, the imitation, of freedom. The state paid lip service to the freedom that had died. It killed freedom and removed its very precious, radioactive vital organs—and then stuffed it as a taxidermist might stuff a dead game bird. Give a savage a complicated instrument like a chronometer or a sextant, and he uses it as a toy or an ornament. In

Stalinist Russian freedom was treated in the same way.

Dead freedom became an ornament of the state, but one not without its uses. Dead freedom became the principal figure in a gigantic stage presentation, in a tremendous puppet show on an unbelievable scale. The state which had no freedom created a stage set complete with parliament, elections, trade unions, and a whole society and social life. In the state without freedom matters already resolved and decisions already reached were ostensibly discussed and concluded on the stage sets of collective farm administrations, the administrations of the Writers Union and the Artists Union, on the stage sets of the presidiums of the district executive committees and the provincial executive committees, on the stage sets of the Comparty bureaus, plenary meetings of the district Comparty committees, provincial Comparty committees, and the central committees of the national Comparties. Even the Presidium of the Central Committee of the Communist Party of the Soviet Union was a stage set, a pantomime theater.

For Stalin such a theater was entirely in character. It was entirely in character, too, for a state without freedom.

What was real and not a stage set? Who actually made the decisions?

What was real was Stalin. The decisions were his. But, of course, he could not personally decide all the questions that arose in the state—whether a teacher named Semyenova should get a vacation, whether the Dawn Collective Farm should plant peas or cabbage.

Even though the principle of the state without freedom demanded that he decide everything himself, this was of course physically impossible, and questions of secondary importance were decided by Stalin's intimates. But they were always decided in Stalin's spirit.

That is the only reason why these men were Stalin's trusted agents or the trusted agents of his trusted agents. Their decisions had one essential in common: whether they involved the construction of hydroelectric power stations on the lower reaches of the Volga or enrolling the famous milkmaid Anyuta Feoktistiva in a two-month course of special studies, they were all made in Stalin's spirit. The essence of the matter was that Stalin's spirit and the spirit of the state were one and the same.

Stalin's trusted agents could immediately be spotted at any meeting, rally, congress: no one ever argued with them. They spoke in the name of Stalin-the-state.

And the fact that the state without freedom always acted in the name of freedom and democracy, that it was afraid to take a step without invoking the name of freedom, bore witness to the strength of freedom. Stalin feared few things, but he feared freedom—constantly, permanently, and to the end of his life. Having killed freedom, he then fawned upon its corpse.

That opinion is mistaken which maintains that the events of collectivization and of Yezhov's ascendancy in 1937 were meaningless expressions of uncontrolled, unlimited power in the hands of a cruel man. In reality, the state required the blood that was shed in 1930 and in 1937. As Stalin used to express it, it was not shed for nothing: it left its mark. Without it the state would not have survived. After all, nonfreedom shed that blood in order to destroy freedom. It was an old, old necessity. It had begun under Lenin.

Freedom was destroyed not only in politics and public

life, but on the farms—in the right to sow freely and freely reap. Freedom was overcome in poetry and philosophy, in shoemaking, in the choice of reading matter, in changing one's residence, in the working conditions of factory workers, whose piece-rates, physical safeguards, and wages were determined wholly by the will of the state.

Nonfreedom triumphed indivisibly from the Pacific Ocean to the Black Sea: everywhere and in everything. And everywhere and in everything freedom was destroyed.

To assure a victorious assault, it had to be carried out with a great deal of bloodshed. After all, freedom is life; thus to destroy freedom Stalin killed life.

Stalin's personality was embodied in the gigantic works of the Five-Year Plans, those thundering pyramids of the twentieth century which corresponded to the sumptuous ancient monuments and palaces of Asia that so enchanted Stalin's soul. Human beings did not need these gigantic structures—any more than God needed huge cathedrals and mosques.

Stalin's character was expressed in the hugely inflated activity of the state security organs he created.

The use of torture in interrogations, the actions of the internal security agents, who destroyed not only individuals but whole classes and strata of people, the methods of search and seizure which had developed in a straight line from Malyuta Skuratov to Count Benkendorf—all these techniques of the punitive apparatus he created found their equivalents in Stalin's soul.

But the most ominous, sinister equivalent of all was the combination in Stalin's nature of the Russian revolutionary tradition with the tradition—also Russian—of an unrestrainedly powerful secret police.

This combination, existing in Stalin's own character and reflected in the security organs he created, had its prototype in the czarist Russian state.

The association of Degayev, the intellectual and narodnaya volya leader who subsequently became an Okhrana agent, with Colonel Sudyeikin, chief police inquisitor, took place in the years when Joseph Djugashvili was a small boy, and it foretold this sinister conjunction.

Sudyeikin, the bright skeptic, the connoisseur and admirer of Russia's revolutionary efforts, sardonically observing the ignorance of the czar and the czarist ministers whom he served, used the narodnaya volya disciple Degayev for his police purposes. And the narodnaya volya disciple Degayev served both the Revolution and the police at one and the same time.

Sudyeikin's plans were not destined to succeed. He hoped that by aiding and abetting the revolutionaries, and then working up faked cases against them, he would frighten the czar, come to power, and become a dictator. As head of the state he would then destroy the Revolution. But his bold dreams were not realized. Degayev killed Sudyeikin.

Stalin, however, succeeded. And somehow—hidden from everyone and even from himself—his victory encompassed the triumph of Sudyeikin's dream of harnessing two horses to one cart: the Revolution and the secret police.

Stalin, born of the Revolution, finished off the revolutionaries with the help of the police apparatus.

And perhaps the persecution mania which so tormented him was aroused by the same secret fear, buried within his subconscious, that Sudyeikin had felt toward Degayev. The revolutionary Degayev, even though abjectly in the power of the secret police, inspired terror in the police chief. And it was particularly horrifying that Sudyeikin and Degayev, traitors, friends, and enemies, lived on together in the crowded murk of Stalin's soul.

Here perhaps, or hereabouts, lies the explanation of the riddle which most baffled observers in 1937: Why was it necessary, when destroying innocent people devoted to the Revolution, to work up and work out the most precise scenarios, false from beginning to end, detailing their participation in cooked-up, imaginary, nonexistent plots?

Subjecting its victims to dreadful tortures that lasted for days, weeks, months, and sometimes years, the state security machine compelled unhappy bookkeepers, engineers, agronomists to play a part in its theatrical productions, to assume the roles of traitors, scoundrels, foreign agents, terrorists, wreckers.

Millions of people have asked why this was done.

After all, when Sudyeikin prepared his frame-ups, he intended to deceive the czar. But Stalin did not have to deceive the czar. He *was* the czar.

Yet, nonetheless, Stalin was in fact attempting to deceive the czar, that czar who, in spite of him, lived in the secret murk of his soul.

The invisible czar continued to live on wherever nonfreedom had indivisibly triumphed. And Stalin to the end of his days feared him and him alone.

Also, to the end of his days, Stalin was unable, with all his bloody violence and tyranny, really to finish off that freedom in whose name the Russian Revolution had begun in February, 1917.

The Asiatic in Stalin's soul tried to cheat and deceive freedom, played sly games with freedom, despairing of annihilating freedom once and for all.

25

After Stalin's death Stalin's cause lived on. Just as, in a different time, Lenin's cause had survived him.

The state Stalin built, the state without freedom, lives on. The power and might of industry, of the armed forces, of the punitive apparatus Stalin created, have not passed from the hands of the Party. Nonfreedom still reigns firmly from sea to sea. The function of all-permeating, omnipresent theater has not changed: the same system of elections prevails; the labor unions are as shackled as they were; the peasants are as enslaved; they are still denied passports and, therefore, freedom of movement; and the intelligentsia continues as before to work brilliantly, and to make a great deal of noise, and to play the lackey. The management of this great nation still operates through push buttons, and the power and the authority of the person who pushes the buttons are just as unlimited.

But, of course, much has inevitably changed. It could not help but change.

The state without freedom has entered on its third phase.

Lenin laid the foundations. Stalin erected the superstructure. And now the state without freedom has been put into operation.

Much that was necessary while it was being built has now become unnecessary. The time has passed when it was essential to destroy the ancient little houses on the construction site. The time for destruction, moving, resettlement, for expelling households from ruined private residences, from shanties and hovels, has gone.

The skyscraper has been filled with new inhabitants. Of course, a good many things remain to be accomplished, but there is no need to continue employing the destructive methods of the former supervisor, the big boss.

The foundation of the skyscraper—nonfreedom—is as immovable as ever.

What will happen next? Is that foundation really as immovable as ever?

Was Hegel right when he said that everything real is rational? Is the inhuman real? Is it rational?

The strength of the people's Revolution which began in 1917 was so great that not even the dictatorial state was carrying out, for its own sake only, its cruel and awful purpose of growth and accumulation; it was, without knowing it, bearing freedom within its womb.

Freedom was coming true—but only in the deepest darkness and secrecy. Across the surface of the earth rolls what is obvious to all, the river sweeping everything in its path. The new national state—the owner of all the countless, inestimable wealth of the nation: factories, atomic piles, all the land; the monolithic proprietor of every living breath—celebrated its victory. The Revolution, it appears, took place for the sake of that state, for the sake of its thousand years of power and triumph.

But the owner, the ruler of half the world, was not merely the gravedigger of freedom.

In spite of Lenin's genius, which had inspired the creation of the new world, freedom was coming true. Freedom was coming true because human beings continued to remain human beings.

For the human being who carried out the Revolution of February, 1917, for the human being who created, at the command of the new state, skyscrapers, and factories, and atomic piles, the only possible outcome was freedom. Because, in creating the new world, the human being remained a human being.

At times Ivan Grigoryevich felt and understood all this clearly, and at times vaguely.

No matter how enormous the skyscrapers, no matter how powerful the cannon, no matter how unlimited the might of the state, no matter how vast its empire, all this was only smoke and mist which would disappear. There remained alive and growing one genuine force alone, consisting of one element only—freedom. To live meant to be a free human being. Not everything real was rational. But everything inhuman was senseless and worthless.

And Ivan Grigoryevich found it quite natural that the word "freedom" had been on his lips when, as a student, he went off to Siberia, and that the word had not disappeared from his mind but lived on there even now.

26

He was all alone in the room, and he was carrying on an imaginary conversation with Anna Sergeyevna. He was talking to her inside his head, and here is what he said to her:

I want you to realize that at the most difficult times of all I used to imagine a woman's embraces and think how wonderful they would be. I thought I could find oblivion in them and be able to forget what I had suffered, and I would feel as though none of the pain had ever happened. But as it turned out, you see, I felt the need of telling you, you in particular, about all of it. And you yourself spent that whole night talking, telling me your story. What has happened, you see, is that it makes us happy to share with each other the burden we share with no one else. When you come home from the hospital, I will tell you about the hour that was the worst of all for me. It was a conversation in a prison cell, at dawn, after I had been interrogated.

The man next to me was named Alexei Samoilovich. He

died soon after. I think he was the most intelligent of all the men I ran into. But his mind was frightening. Not because it was evil, you understand, for evil in itself is not frightening. And, for that matter, he did not have an evil mind, but only a mind indifferent to and derisive of faith. He frightened me, he exerted a very strong gravitational force on me. And he refused to accept my faith in freedom.

His life had worked out badly. But it was a life like many others there. He was imprisoned under Section 58–10, the most common of all sections.

He had a powerful brain. His thought would bear me along like a wave, and I used to shudder as a beach might shudder when that wave crashed.

I was brought back to my cell after being interrogated. What a list one could make of the techniques of violence employed throughout history: burning at the stake, prison, and now the new technology of annihilation! Tall and enormous prison fortresses, as large as fair-sized cities, and, of course, camps. Capital punishment began with an oak club crushing the skull, with a rope noose. But today the executioner just turns on the meat grinder and executes one hundred, a thousand, ten thousand people. He no longer even has to swing his ax. Our century is the century of the greatest violence ever committed against the human being by the state. But it is precisely here that the strength and hope of mankind lie. It is the twentieth century that has at last shaken the Hegelian concept of the historical process: "Everything real is rational." It was this concept, violently debated for decades, that Russian thinkers of the past century finally accepted.

But now, at the height of the state's triumph over individual freedom, Russian thinkers wearing padded camp jackets have dethroned and cast down the old Hegelian law and have proclaimed their new, supreme, guiding principle of world history:

"Everything inhuman is senseless and worthless."

Yes, indeed! Amidst the total triumph of inhumanity, it has become self-evident that everything effected by violence is senseless and worthless, and that it has no future and will disappear without a trace.

This is my faith, and with it I would return to my cell after an interrogation. And my bunkmate would usually say to me:

"Why defend freedom? Long ago, people saw in it the law and the meaning of progress. And now, they say, everything is clear: there is no such thing as historical development. History is a molecular process. The human being is equal to himself. Nothing can be done with him. There is no progress. And the law in all this is very simple—the law of the conservation of violence. It is as simple as the law of the conservation of energy. Violence is eternal, no matter what is done to destroy it. It will not disappear and it will not diminish but will only be transformed. It once took the form of slavery. Then of the Mongol invasion. It moves from continent to continent, and sometimes it takes a class form and then is transformed into a racial form. From the material sphere it slips into medieval religiosity. Sometimes it is exercised against the colored races, sometimes against writers and artists, but as an entity its total quantity is constant. Only the chaotic course of its transformations deceives the philosophers, who mistakenly interpret them as evolution, the laws of which they then search for. But chaos has no laws of development, or meaning and content, or goal and purpose. It was Gogol, Russia's genius, who sang of the 'flying troika,' who prophesied the future in its flight, but it was not in Gogol's troika that the future lay. Here is your troika: Russia's bureaucratic destiny, the face-less troika, the three-man special sessions of the NKVD, the troika that sentences people to camp and to be shot, the troika that made up the lists of those who were liquidated as kulaks, the troika that excluded certain young people from the universities, the troika that refused ration cards to old women from the old regime."

And he would continue—waving his threatening finger at Gogol from his bunk:

"You were wrong, Nikolai Vasilyevich, you failed to understand or to envision our flying troika. The history of human beings lies not in the flight of the troika but in chaos and the eternal transformation of one aspect of violence into another. The troika flies, but the human being is motionless and stagnant. The main thing about him is that he is static. His fate is static. Violence is eternal—no matter what is done to destroy it. And the troika flies along and cares nothing for our Russian grief. And what difference does it make to our Russian grief—whether the troika flies or whether it is frozen stock-still?

"And so it turns out that it is not Gogol's troika, but the one that is here with us now, that sits somewhere up there signing death sentences."

And I lay there half-dead on the bunk and the only thing still left alive in me was my faith: the history of human beings is the history of freedom, from less to more; the history of all life, from the amoeba to the human race, is the history of freedom, the transition from less freedom to more freedom; yes, and life itself is freedom too. And this faith gave me strength. I was exploring that precious, marvelous and bright thought which was hidden away in prison rags: "Everything inhuman is senseless and worthless."

And Alexei Samoilovich heard me out, half-alive as I was, and he said:

"You're just fooling yourself with hogwash. The history of life is the history of violence triumphant. It is eternal and indestructible. It may pass through various transformations, but it neither diminishes nor disappears. Yes, and the word 'history' itself has been dreamed up by men. There is no history—it is like grinding water. It is nonsense. The human being does not develop from lower to higher. He is as stationary as a granite cliff. His goodness, his mind, are immovable. The human and humane element does not increase within the human being. What kind of history can human beings have if their goodness is static?"

And I felt overwhelmed—worse than I had ever felt or had ever imagined I could feel. I lay there on my bunk and I thought, "Good Lord! This insufferable pain has been inflicted on me by an intelligent man." And it was like being shot. And I found it unbearable even to breathe. I wanted to die. But my relief came from the most unexpected quarter—they dragged me off again to interrogation. They weren't going to let me have time to catch my breath. And I felt relieved. I believed again in the inevitability of freedom.

The hell with the troika that flies and thunders and signs death sentences. Freedom and Russia will become one!

Do you hear me? When are you going to leave the hospital and come back to me?

Such was his imaginary conversation with Anna Sergeyevna—which never took place.

On a winter day he bade farewell to Anna Sergeyevna at the cemetery. He never did have the chance to share with her what he had remembered, thought about, and written down during the months of her illness.

He took her things to the village, where he spent the day with Alyesha, and then once again returned to his work in the artel.

27

In the autumn Ivan Grigoryevich journeyed to the seaside city near which, in the shadow of a green mountain, his father's home had stood.

The train traveled along the shore, and Ivan Grigoryevich left the railway car during a short stop and looked at the green and black water, always in motion and smelling cool and salty.

The sea and the wind had kept right on, right there, when the interrogator had been working him over at nighttime interrogations, when they had been digging a grave for a zek who died on a prisoner transport, when the police dogs had been barking beneath the barracks windows and the snow had been creaking beneath the camp guards' feet.

The sea was eternal, and the eternity of its freedom seemed to Ivan Grigoryevich akin to indifference. The sea was unconcerned with Ivan Grigoryevich when he went to live beyond the Arctic Circle, and the sea would be unconcerned with him when he stopped living. He thought: this is not freedom; this is interstellar space come down to earth, a fragment of eternity, always in motion, indifferent.

The sea is not freedom. But it is in the likeness of freedom. It is the symbol. How beautiful is freedom itself if the mention of it, if its likeness, fills a man with happiness.

He reboarded the train. Reaching his destination, he spent the night at the station, and early in the morning went off in the direction of his father's house. The autumn sun hung in the cloudless heavens, and it was no different from the spring sun.

He walked along in a sleepy, empty stillness. He felt such great emotion welling up within him that it seemed as though his heart, that had withstood everything else, would this time finally give out. The world, as he walked, became divinely still; the blessed peace of his childhood was eternal and immutable. His feet had once trod these cool cobblestones. His childish eyes had once looked at these rounded mountains touched with the red of autumn's rust. He listened to the rush of the stream hurrying to the sea with the debris of the city—watermelon rinds and corncobs.

Along the street, in the direction of the bazaar, went an old Abkhazian man in a black sateen blouse, belted with a thin leather belt. He was carrying a basket of chestnuts.

Perhaps in his childhood Ivan Grigoryevich had bought chestnuts and figs from this very same, changeless old man. And this southern morning air had been the same: so cool and warm, smelling of the sea and of the mountain sky, and with the kitchen odor of garlic in it too. And these little houses, too, with their closed gates, their curtains drawn. Perhaps the children of forty years ago, not grown old, were sleeping behind the same closed shutters; perhaps the same old men were there, too, not yet gone to their graves.

He emerged on the highway and began to climb the

mountain. The stream roared. Ivan Grigoryevich remembered its voice.

He had never ever seen all his life as a whole, and now suddenly he could see it.

And, as he saw it, he felt no anger against anyone.

All of them—those who had driven him, pushing him along with a gunstock, to the interrogator's cabinet, and those who would not let him sleep during interrogations, and those who had said loathsome things about him while they were being interrogated, those who had said repulsive things about him at meetings and assemblies, those who had renounced him, those who had stolen his camp bread, those who had beaten him—all of them, in all their weakness, rudeness, crudeness, malice, had not done him evil because they really wanted to.

They had betrayed, slandered, renounced him because one could not get along otherwise, one could not survive otherwise. And yet they were human beings. Could any of them really have wanted him to be making his way thus to his abandoned home—old, lonely, loveless?

People wished no one harm, yet throughout their lives people did harm to others.

Nonetheless, human beings were human beings. And it was a marvelous, divine thing, because, whether they wanted to or not, they were not allowing freedom to die, and even the most awful and terrible among them nurtured freedom in their awful, distorted, warped, yet human souls.

He had achieved nothing in life. He would leave behind him no books, no paintings, no discoveries. He had created no school of thought, no political party, and he had no pupils or followers.

Why had his life been so hard? He had not preached nor

had he taught—he had remained exactly what he had been from his birth: a human being.

The slope of the mountain opened before him. From behind the pass the peaks of the oak trees showed. In his childhood, he had gone there into the forest twilight, and searched out the remnants of the vanished life of the Circassians—the fruit trees gone wild, the traces of the fences around their obliterated houses.

Perhaps his own home was still standing there just as changelessly as the streets and the stream seemed changeless.

Here was one more bend of the road. For a moment, it seemed to him as if an impossibly bright light, brighter than any he had ever seen in his life, had flooded the earth. A few steps more and in this light he would see that home, and his mother would come out to meet him, her prodigal son, and he would kneel down before her, and her young and beautiful hands would lie upon his gray, balding head.

He saw the thickets of thorns and hops. There was nothing left of the house nor of the well—only a few stones that shone white in the dusty grass, burned by the sun.

He stood there—gray, bent, and changeless.

1955–1963

About the Author

Vasily Grossman was a Soviet writer of Russian Jewish background who was very popular with Soviet intellectuals. Born in 1905 in Berdichev, he graduated from the physics and mathematics faculty of Moscow University in 1929. He worked in the Donbass for some years as a chemical engineer and expert on workers' safety precautions. His first novella, "Glyukauf," appeared in the journal, *Literary Donbass,* in 1934. His 1934 story, "In the City of Berdichev," which dealt with an episode from the time of the Civil War, attracted the attention of Maxim Gorky. Gorky took the young author under his protection and arranged for the publication of "Glyukauf" in a revised version in the almanac *The Nineteenth Year.* Grossman's lengthy novel, *Stepan Kolchugin,* about a young worker in a mining settlement who matured to become a revolutionary, was published in four parts in 1937–40. During World War II Grossman was a war correspondent at the front for *Red Star,* producing brilliant war journals and fine reporting.

In 1946 his play *If You Believe the Pythagoreans* was published in Moscow and bitterly attacked by the most authoritative and the most vicious of the Party literary critics, V. V. Yermilov. Grossman fell victim to more violent criticism because of his Jewish origin during the bitter campaign against the "homeless cosmopolites" in 1949. In 1952 the first part of *For a Just Cause,* Grossman's war epic, was published in *Novy Mir.* It was scathingly attacked in *Pravda* in February, 1953, shortly before Stalin's death. In the upshot Grossman never completed the novel. The persecution of the period from 1946 to 1953 evidently left a lasting mark on him. He was at work on *Forever Flowing* from 1955 to 1963. He died September 14, 1964.